THE ROAD to CAMELOT

A Random House book
Published by Random House Australia Pty Ltd
Level 3, 100 Pacific Highway, North Sydney NSW 2060
www.randomhouse.com.au

First published by Random House Australia in 2002
This edition published 2009

Addresses for companies within the Random House Group can be found at
www.randomhouse.com.au/offices.

Cataloguing-in-Publication Entry for this book is available from the
National Library of Australia

ISBN 978 1 86471 948 2

Cover design by www.blacksheep-uk.com
Cover photography by Superstock
Typeset in 13/17 Joanna by Asset Typesetting Pty Ltd
Printed and bound by Griffin Press, South Australia

Random House Australia uses papers that are natural, renewable and recyclable
products and made from wood grown in sustainable forests. The logging and
manufacturing processes are expected to conform to the environmental regulations
of the country of origin.

10 9 8 7 6 5 4 3 2 1

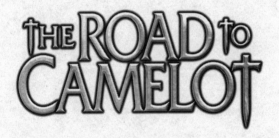

THE ROAD TO CAMELOT

EDITED BY
SOPHIE MASSON

RANDOM HOUSE AUSTRALIA

CONTENTS

INTRODUCTION

the history and development
of the Arthurian legend

Sophie Masson

If ever there was a defining story of Western culture, it is that of Arthur Pendragon, King of the Isles: *rex quondam, rex futuris*, or the once and future king. Part action-packed, magical adventure and spiritual exploration, part complex human tragedy and rich evocation of an enchanted world-view, this richly hybrid, multilayered, multicultural and extraordinarily potent legend of the great king, his court at Camelot and his Knights of the Round Table lies at the base of a great deal of the way in which we still see ourselves. And it has within it much that we can still learn from.

The legend is huge, and comprises many, many stories, but the basic thread is this: a young orphaned boy named Arthur, who has been brought up by a foster-father, Sir Ector, comes as a squire to his foster-brother Kay, to the court of the late King of Logres, Uther Pendragon. There sits a sword magically inserted into a stone, which can only be drawn by the one who will be king. Arthur draws it — and learns that he is actually the son of Uther, and the next king. He also learns that he is under the protection of the great wizard Merlin, who is also a prophet, and who tells him of his strange birth, and of the fact that he has two half-sisters, Morgause and the enchantress Morgan (sometimes written Morgana, Morgana le Fay, or Morgaine).

Arthur, with Merlin at his side, spends much time in the next few years building an army of loyal and heroic young men, many of them also orphaned, and fighting back the warlords who have made his country of Logres into a wasteland. Once he has beaten the warlords and restored peace in the country, he builds Camelot, the great city where all will know peace and prosperity. As well, he founds the Fellowship of the Round Table, where sit his companions, the greatest knights in all the world, who help him keep Camelot safe. Such knights as Gawain, Lancelot, Galahad, Tristan, Perceval, Bors, Kay and more join the Round Table. As well, Arthur is given a magic sword,

Excalibur, by one of his Otherworldly friends, the Lady of the Lake. He also meets and marries Guinevere, the beautiful, strong-willed daughter of a neighbouring king. And for a while, all seems well.

Unfortunately, Lancelot, who has been brought up by the Lady of the Lake, arrives in Camelot, meets Guinevere and falls madly in love with her, and she with him. Their doomed love will be a part of the eventual breakdown of Camelot, and the end of the fellowship of the Round Table. But there are other reasons, too, for its end, for Arthur has dark secrets of his own. Through enchantment, long ago he slept, without knowing it, with his half-sister Morgause, the mother of Gawain, Agravain, Gaheris and Gareth, all Round Table knights, and fathered a child, Mordred. Unloved, Mordred is brought up by Arthur's other sister, the enchantress Morgana le Fay, and schooled in the hatred of his father. Eventually, Mordred comes to court — and the beginning of the downfall of Camelot, and the reign of Arthur, commences. At the end, Arthur is mortally wounded in a great battle, but, reconciled to Morgana, he is taken by his sister and the Lady of the Lake to a wonderful island called Avalon where no-one will ever die. It is said he is not dead, but merely sleeping, waiting for the call to come again.

This is a very, very basic outline of the story, which includes many extraordinary stories and parts, with fantastic, moving, exciting and action-packed adventures as well as great tragedies and spiritual journeys. There are some wonderful retellings of the legend, and I have included these in the Further Reading section at the end of this book. There are also many different versions of the stories, for instance in some, Morgause is Gawain's mother, in other's it is Morgana.

Was there ever a 'real' King Arthur? No-one knows for sure. There have been plenty of theories about the historical background of the story, and it seems clear that the fifth or sixth centuries are probably the time-frame in which a 'real' Arthur might well have existed. This was the time during the collapse of the Roman Empire when Roman armies, recalled to defend Rome itself, had left the Romano-Celtic colonies in Britain and Gaul (France) undefended against the onslaughts of Germanic invaders such as the Angles, Saxons, Jutes, Goths, Visigoths, Vandals, and so on. Local communities had to defend themselves against these invaders, and so defensive associations were formed, some of which succeeded, at least for a time, in repelling the invasions and keeping the peace that had once been a feature of Romano-Celtic life.

A king who could unite his people, push back chaos and restore the peace, prosperity and rich cultural life that had been their experience and was now their dream, would be a great hero indeed, forever remembered. Such was the background. And several real historical figures of the time could have been the model for such a longed-for dream, but we are not sure if any of them was in fact the actual source for the 'real' Arthur. There have been many books written on this subject as well, and in the Further Reading section, I have noted down a few for those with an interest in the historical Arthur.

However, as well as history there is, of course, a great deal of myth in the legend. Much of this myth is Celtic, though there are also Roman, Middle Eastern, Germanic, Viking, Scythian and other elements present in some of it. What is certain is that the earliest documented versions of the legend occurred in Britain, especially in that part of it we call Wales, where the original Breton or British tongue of pre-Roman Britain was still spoken (and incidentally, is still spoken), but also in England and Scotland. These stories are not well known or familiar to the great majority of people, though: there is no Merlin, no Lancelot, no Galahad, and so on, in them, and although there's a deal of magic, it occurs in an offhand, typically Celtic, sort of way. In these early stories there's certainly no discussion of idealism or the torments of adulterous love, as there was later. Nevertheless, the compelling presence of the magical Celtic Otherworld is probably the single most important factor why the Arthurian legend began to take off so spectacularly in the rest of Europe.

The first Arthurian story boom occurred over more

than three hundred years, from the beginning of the twelfth to the end of the fifteenth century. This is from where most of the stories and the characters we know and love have come. This is where we meet Merlin, and Morgana le Fay, and Lancelot, and Gawain, and Galahad, and Tristan and Iseult, and myriad other characters from the court of Camelot and beyond. We find in these medieval stories the complex portrait of Arthur and the triple tragedy of Arthur, Lancelot and Guinevere; the knights' journeys into the magical forest and their adventures there, the ordeal through Castle Perilous, the reblooming of the Waste Land, the Quest for the Grail, the treachery of Mordred, the end — and yet not quite the end — in the blessed island of Avalon.

Geoffrey of Monmouth, the twelfth-century Welsh historian writing for the Norman rulers of England, may well have set one of the seeds of the Arthurian boom with his famous *History of the Kings of Britain*. But equally important were the innumerable humble bards and minstrels and 'jongleurs' of British or Breton origin, who crisscrossed western Europe in this great restless age of travel and pilgrimage and the gathering of new influences and new ideas. And so the word spread among ordinary people, as well as the great ones of this world, in England and France and Aquitaine and Germany and Italy and Spain. To call a tale 'Breton' as to call it 'Celtic' now, became a buzzword, a sure-fire recipe for success, and many people wanted to get on this lucrative bandwagon. But in the work of the great medieval writers — Chretien de Troyes, Marie de France, Wolfram von Eschenbach, Robert de Boron, Thomas Malory, and many others, including a great many anonymous writers — we come face to face with that mixture of the mundane and the marvellous, of wit and wonder, savagery and spirituality, psychological truth and wild adventure, which is the hallmark of the high Middle Ages.

One of the extraordinary things about the Arthurian legend is that its massive European success was more or less created by women. The new cult of Woman: Sacred Woman, the Virgin Mary; and Secular Woman: the Beloved, was a powerful undertone to many of the twelfth-century stories. Honour, chivalry, courtesy, civility, frankness, boldness, and love between equals: these did not exactly replace the old male heroic code, but added depth and complexity to it. These new ideals were promoted by such extraordinary people as the brilliant ruler Eleanor of Aquitaine, and her daughter, the equally cultured Marie, Countess of Champagne, who was Chretien de Troyes' patron, as well as by the prolific and remarkable Marie de France, the first woman poet to write in the French language. The twelfth century was a time when women were often left alone to manage estates and families: not only great ladies, but ordinary farming women too, and townswomen, because their menfolk had rushed off to the Crusades or on pilgrimages. And so we find that many, if not all, of the Arthurian heroes in the medieval stories are fatherless, in one way or the other, and must take their place in the world, and understand their own journey in life with female guides and mentors from the Otherworld. Arthur is the prime example of this, but other figures from the legend, such as Lancelot, Perceval, Gawain, Galahad, Merlin, even Mordred, all share in it. This is a society of young male peers, coached into honour and the right way by women.

The motif of the Grail Quest, which became immensely popular, first saw the light in continental Europe in Chretien de Troyes' lovely story of Perceval, itself based on the Welsh story of Peredur. Here, the nature of the Grail is very much left vague: it is not, as it becomes later, a specifically Christian symbol. By the mid-thirteenth century, however, when the Arthurian craze showed no sign of diminishing, the monkish scribes had decided to take part in it too. And so, many more stories were written where the Christian symbolism was clarified and heightened, and some of the stories showed an unpleasant monkish tendency to misogyny. But even they could not wreck the notion of the Grail Quest, which is most importantly a symbolic journey of the human soul, through all of life's tests and challenges and ordeals, to full integration as a human being and as a child of God. The quest was seen as a hopeful one at first, but Sir Thomas Malory, the last, and to many the greatest of the medieval Arthurian writers, writing at a time of personal torment, and in the transitional time of the fifteenth century, emphasised very much the yearning note of melancholy and nostalgia and guilt that the Arthurian legend has carried ever since.

Then the legend fell into disrepute and neglect for three centuries; but in the nineteenth century, it came back with a vengeance. Writers such as Alfred Lord Tennyson and the Pre-Raphaelite painters made Arthur's story, and those of his companions, enormously popular again. Today, the new Arthurian boom, already nearly two centuries old, shows no sign of diminishing. Books on Arthur proliferate; the original medieval documents are there for all to peruse, there are many scholars throughout the world examining every aspect of the history and literature and mythological basis of the legend, and debates rage across the world.

Dotty theories abound, as do serious scholarly tomes. Meanwhile, creative writers all over the world and throughout the century have taken Arthurian influences directly and indirectly into their work. These include CS Lewis, TS Eliot, John Steinbeck, Kevin Crossley-Holland, TH White, Rosemary Sutcliff, Raymond Chandler, Marion Zimmer Bradley, Guy Gavriel Kay, Alan Garner, JRR Tolkien, JK Rowling, Haydn Middleton, Lindsay Clarke, Lloyd Alexander,

Philip Reeve, Peter Dickinson, Susan Cooper, Anthony Burgess, Robertson Davies, Mary Stewart and Michael Morpurgo, to mention only a tiny number. Many genres, such as fantasy and much detective fiction, owe an enormous debt to the Arthurian legend and the template of Camelot and its emblematic knights, policing the edges of darkness and protecting the light, sometimes against overwhelming odds.

Film's full of it, from the overtly Arthurian, such as Eric Rohmer's *Perceval le Gallois* (1978), John Boorman's *Excalibur* (1981), Jerry Zucker's *First Knight* (1995), Antoine Fuqua's *King Arthur* (2004), and Kevin Reynolds' *Tristan and Isolde* (2006), to such Arthurian-influenced cultural icons as the western and science fiction and fantasy films including *Star Wars*, *Galaxy Quest* and *Star Trek*. TV also loves Arthur, with shows ranging from the creative use of the Arthurian stories in the Canadian–Australian *Guinevere Jones* series (2002) and the BBC's hit series *Merlin* (2008) to many documentaries exploring the historical roots of the legend. Many musicians have also been influenced, from rock band Led Zeppelin to the brilliant Canadian multi-talented group La Nef, with their original and compelling musical setting of Chretien's Perceval and the Quest for the Grail, and fellow Canadian Loreena McKennitt's haunting setting of Tennyson's 'The Lady of Shalott'. But it's not only the arts which embrace Arthur: even that tarnished arena, politics, has used some of its terms: don't we talk of John F Kennedy's reign as Camelot? In fact, the present reign in the west of peace and prosperity may itself be seen as a kind of Camelot, always having to be protected from the incursions of its enemies.

Take a glance at the net, and you will see how many Arthurian sites there are; and the New Age movement is full of Arthurian allusions, too. Indeed, there are people running workshops based on Arthurian legends used as therapy! If each age has its own Arthur, its own take on the legend, our age has brought women back to the fore in a big way: not only are the female characters in modern Arthurian fiction goddesses and coaches, guides and partners, now they can be adventurers too!

And what of Australia, with our reputation for dun-coloured realism? Is there any place in our tough, disillusioned culture for the Arthurian legend? Well, yes, and plenty. Indeed, Australians are just as moved and influenced by this great legend as people anywhere else taking part in the magical, evolving adventure of culture. Funnily enough, the Antipodes is pinpointed in some medieval literature as being the 'real' Avalon!

There are many Australian writers who have used specifically Arthurian allusions in their work, from poet Peter Kocan's moving explorations of Arthurian characters to novelist Jessica Anderson's *Tirra Lirra by the River*, based on the Lady of Shalott, and Alan Gould's *The Tazyrik Year*, based on Sir Gawain and the Green Knight, to my own *Forest of Dreams*, set in the twelfth century and based on the life and work of poet Marie de France. In children's literature,

Felicity Pulman's wonderful *Shalott* series explores a new way of looking at the themes and emotions behind the story of Elaine of Astolat and her doomed love for Lancelot, who has eyes only for Guinevere.

And now, of course, there is *The Road to Camelot*, where fourteen of Australia's best writers of fantasy have delved into the childhoods and adolescences of some of the legend's most memorable characters. Each writer has put his or her unique perspective on the way in which a hero or heroine — or even villain — is formed when they are young, and what experiences may lead them to take on their destiny and to begin to understand who they are. Their brief was to explore those characters at a point of crisis or decision in their lives; there were no limits put on time-frame or cultural background and so many different versions of the legends were used. Some writers have chosen the dangerous and tumultuous period in which a historical Arthur might have been likely to operate, others have chosen the more settled and pleasant atmosphere of the high Middle Ages, others have chosen a timeless period or a more modern flavour. What mattered most was the essence of each character — their humanity, their individuality. For that is one of the essential appeals of the legend of Arthur: its understanding of our common humanity, our mixture of comedy and tragedy, our divided nature, our hopes and our fears, our loves and our hatreds. And most of all, how we live our lives.

ꟿꟾ ERLIN

Maggie Hamilton

I t had happened again. The same terrifying dream filled with the confused cries of women and children, and the impatient scream of horses. One minute he and Dinabutius were at each other, fists raised, and the next the soldiers were on him, their calloused hands about his neck and shoulders. Already he was as tall as they, but he had not their brutish strength. As he fought the mounting terror that tore through his captive limbs, he smelt the unmistakable stench of death.

They meant to kill him!

Merlin shot up from his sleep-warmed pallet, his

skin drenched with sweat. It was only as he stared through the darkness at the dying embers in the firepit that he realised he had crossed the thin line between waking and sleep. As he ran his fingers through his waistlength hair, he lost himself in the blood-red flames. What forces were abroad that could disturb him so?

He was bone weary from the endless visions that had pursued him of late. More than anything he wanted them to cease, but even as he wished, the future beckoned once more. He could see many men, hundreds of them, their weapons raised as they ran to their deaths across a windswept plain. Merlin shuddered to see the deadly flight of spears darken an already stormy sky. Turning swiftly to one side he shut his eyes tight, but it made no difference, still the terrible scene continued to unfold. The deep silence of the night was shattered by the roar of battle, by the clash of sword upon sword and the agonised cries of wounded men and beasts.

The flood tide was coming that would destroy the world as they knew it.

His first impulse was to snatch up his few possessions and take to the road. And why not? He had no kin or craft to bind him to this place. Yet he knew that no matter where he fled his fate was sure to follow. Clutching at his threadbare blanket, Merlin struggled to his feet and dragged himself to the mouth of the cave.

Then he pushed aside the ancient wolfskin and stepped outside to welcome the immediate bite of the cold on his hands and face. It was only then, as he breathed in huge lungsful of fresh air, that the nightmarish vision ceased.

The sweet relief of it!

For as long as he could remember, Merlin had been able to read the hearts and minds of those around him, to see those whom death stalked and those who bore the beginnings of sickness. But now his sight was propelling him further and with such force that he feared where it might lead. He did not doubt that his was indeed a gift from the gods, but it came at a high price.

From the first, his Sight had marked him out as one to be wary of. To be merely a bastard might have been bearable, but to be marked as one of the devil's brood was another thing altogether, and time and again the ignorant and the cruel had sought him out, their thoughless remarks cutting him as surely as any knife.

It was no accident that Merlin had finally abandoned Camarthen for his cave on the hill. He needed the freedom to live as he chose, and this was only possible when he was able to live apart from those whose minds were narrow and whose hearts were fickle. Not that he lacked company. Still the townspeople would wend their way up to his simple abode to gain his assistance in matters of sickness or love. He, in turn, was happy to share the gifts of his healing hands and his knowledge of herbal lore, but he steadfastly refused to manipulate the forces around him or to glimpse into the future in any way. To be in possession of such awesome powers as were his terrified him. They were more than any mortal man could bear, and sooner or later he feared that madness would follow.

But now, as Merlin stood in the clearing outside the cave, he allowed himself to become one with the silence. It never failed to inspire him, and to feed him body and soul. He was ever grateful for the solitude of his hillside retreat, and for the many precious plants and trees, for the ancient rocks and hidden springs, and the abundance of birds and beasts. Over time they had become his friends and teachers, rewarding his gentleness and patient observation many times over. Here on this lone hill these many living things had thrived for generations, untouched by the chaotic affairs of men, and here they would remain long after he and others were gone.

Merlin let out a long sigh as he gazed up at the sliver of moon that hung insubstantial as a thread amid the glittering dark of the night sky. Then, as he lost himself in the welcome expanse of the heavens he dreamt of another time and place, of a long forgotten isle with gold-topped palaces and temples, girt by turquoise seas. There, in that fantastic kingdom amid exotic birds and gardens and the soothing melodies of the harp and flute he remained, until he was roused by the quiet pad of a fox on its way home from a kill. Tired now he retreated to his bed, where he fell into a deep, dreamless sleep.

Over the ensuing weeks, many of the haunting visions faded and his life became peaceful once more. The last vestiges of autumn gave way to the stark beauty of winter, which in turn was followed by an indifferent spring. Then on a rare day when there was a little warmth to be had in the sun, Merlin ventured into Camarthen for some black bread and oatcakes, and a horn or two of honey mead.

His steps were light as he wandered through the maze of narrow streets. At the centre of the market was a cluster of makeshift stalls selling brilliantly dyed cloths, fleeces and skins, candles and cups, and strips of leather to braid the hair. And scattered among the stalls were hastily constructed pens that housed pigs and chickens and geese.

People from outlying districts were busy haggling over their bundles of dry wood and rushes, and their neatly stacked squares of peat, while the merchants who had travelled far were able to name their price as they traded salt, or necklets and anklets of polished copper and stone. In the midst of the bustle and the chatter the womenfolk scurried from stall to stall weighing up the merits of a little more for the table, or something to grace their wrists or their neck, while the men gathered together to argue or to occupy themselves at dice.

It had been many moons since Merlin had ventured so far, and he was surprised at how much he was enjoying the lively exchanges, yet as soon as he caught the smell of cooked meat, nothing else could hold his attention. Following his nose he made his way past a pile of woven baskets and traps and a tinker sharpening knives, and arrived at a tiny stall where an elderly couple were huddled over their pots of broth and stewed mutton. After months of simple fare Merlin was transfixed by the many bewitching aromas that filled the air. He was still deciding whether to spend what little he had on some broth when his cloak was wrenched from his shoulders.

Spinning round he found himself face to face with Dinabutius, his old tormentor, whose vile temper was equalled only by his evil tongue. Merlin's heart sank to see his adversary's cheeks flushed with ale. Eager to be gone he bent to retrieve his cloak, but before he could do so Dinabutius seized the advantage and punched him about the head and neck. Unprepared for this sudden attack, Merlin sank to his knees. It had been a long time since he had seen Dinabutius, but he was clearly no less vicious.

His hands raised in defence, Merlin kept his eyes fixed on his opponent. Even though Dinabutius was drunk, he was still strong as an ox. Moving deftly from side to side, Merlin managed to avoid the worst of the blows as he scrambled back to his feet. Enraged to see Merlin upright, Dinabutius lunged forward doubly determined to exact what injury he could.

Not daring to employ his magical arts to assist him in so public a place, Merlin had no other choice than to seek a physical means of escape, but as he glanced wildly about him he soon realised he had little cause to be hopeful. Already he was cut off by a tight circle of onlookers crowding in upon them, their hands making swift signs of protection as they waited eagerly to see what would happen next.

Buoyed up by all this attention Dinabutius swaggered about lashing out at Merlin at every turn. Then, without warning there was a sudden break in the crowd. Merlin pushed past his assailant and made for the gap, but before he could reach it he was aware of the sound of horses. Wherever they were going, they were clearly in a hurry. And then he heard the cries of women and children as soldiers forced their way through the crowd.

In that instant Merlin's dream returned to him with an awful clarity. Even before the men reached him he knew that they had come for him, and that there was murder in their hearts. He fought with everything he had to try to escape, but he was no match for their strength. In no time his hands were bound and he was being taken before the High King.

Although his garb was little better than that of a beggar's, Merlin stood before Vortigern as an equal, his azure eyes holding the space between them without fear or judgment. The mighty king stared back at him, searching the young stranger's features for some sign of weakness. There was none. Impressed by this, Vortigern ordered Merlin's hands be loosed.

Merlin acknowledged the gesture with a slight bow, then waited to see what might transpire. While he knew his life hung in the balance he did not fear death, because he knew its shadowy landscape well. Merlin also knew that he belonged to the gods, and that they and they alone knew the time and place of his death.

Never taking his eyes from Vortigern, he let a part of himself dissolve, and as he did so time stretched, allowing him to sense the mood of the place. He was intrigued to meet Vortigern, who, while devious and cruel, was every inch the conqueror. On his right arm he bore the symbol of the dragon and about his powerful neck lay a twisted band of gold. All the many hardships the man had endured on the road to victory were writ on his powerful frame, which was lean and scarred with battle.

And there surrounding Vortigern were his many soldiers and serving men. There, too, were his wizards and soothsayers, who had been summoned to explain the lack of progress that had been made on the construction of his hill fort. Yet in spite of all they professed, they had not the powers to discern the misfortunes, natural or otherwise, that had befallen that ill-fated place. In their desperation and ignorance they had told Vortigern that his fort would never be built unless they found a male who had no mortal father, killed him, and sprinkled the foundation stones with his blood.

Suddenly Merlin caught sight of a holy woman standing some distance away. His breath caught in his throat, for he realised who she was.

How could he have missed her?

In that same instant, she turned towards him as if drawn by an invisible thread, and as Merlin's heart beat painfully against his chest, he found himself staring into a face that was as familiar to him as his own. That of his mother, the Princess, now a nun. Even after all her years of sacred confinement, Demetius' daughter bore herself royally. Beautiful she was, and young still.

Forgetting herself his mother stepped towards him, her arms raised. Uncertain of how best to greet her

Merlin straightened, wishing he had something fitting to wear and that his hair was combed and bound. No sooner was this thought loosed, than her response was swimming joyously inside his head.

'Sweet heaven, it takes my breath away to look upon you,' she assured him, her eyes brilliant with tears. Then she leant forward and stroked his cheek with her forefinger, and as her flesh touched his all the years of bitter loneliness dissolved.

It seemed to Merlin that this dreamlike moment had no beginning or end. And in it his mother was joined by a princely man who was dressed in garments so fine they looked as if they were made of spun gold. Here with his mother was one whose peerless soul matched her own. While this otherworldly prince visited Merlin often in his dreams, only now did the youth realise this was his own father.

To see his parents together after so long was almost more than Merlin could bear, but then as he looked at them, each in turn, he realised that theirs was the kind of love that is accessible only to those rare souls who are both pure and profoundly wise. Now at last Merlin understood why his mother had removed herself from the world. How else might a woman as gifted as she commune freely with her beloved and with the many realms that existed beyond this?

Then as the vast ocean of his parents' love reached out to him, Merlin was shown that long before this time his parents had chosen to light the way for him, so that he might succeed on his difficult quest. Seeking now to honour them, he bowed low before his father, then gathered his mother in his arms, kissing her solemnly on the forehead. Here in the wombtime of existence they remained talking of many things until time folded in on itself, and Merlin and his mother found themselves back in the realm of forgetfulness, two subjects standing before the king.

'Is this thy son?' asked Vortigern, his harsh voice piercing the joy that now danced between them.

Merlin's mother gave a slight nod, her face lit with a fierce pride.

'How then was this lad begot?' asked the king.

A flicker of fear crossed her face and was gone. There beside her once more was her *daimon* lover, visible only to herself and her son.

'What of thy son's father?' pressed the king.

In spite of her lover's encouragement, still the princess hestitated. How could she explain the awesome beauty of the realms of light to those who knew little more than waking and sleep? But then, as her elfin prince placed his hands about her slender shoulders, she was able to draw sufficient strength from him to talk of the many things that had long remained unspoken.

'By my troth, my *daimon* love would visit me in my bower whenever I was alone,' she confessed. 'His words fell upon my virgin heart like gentle rain, and his touch was like none other, but it was the awesome beauty of his soul that captured my love. To be with him was to stand at the very gates of heaven.'

Entranced by all the princess recounted, Vortigern remained silent for a long time. He had not the words to describe how his soul ached to be in the presence of such goodness. He remembered once more the honeyed lips of Ronnwen and her lusty embrace. Much he had sacrificed for his Saxon beauty, and every part of him cried out to be reminded of this. It opened up within him a well of pain so deep that he longed to free himself of all he possessed, including his kingship, which hung like a millstone around his neck.

He looked at Merlin, and was struck by the extraordinary intelligence in his eyes. Impulsively setting aside any idea of killing the young stranger, Vortigern chose instead to explain the many ills that had befallen the construction of his new hill fort.

When Vortigern had finished, an unwelcome silence descended. Although Merlin could straight away have told the king everything he needed to know and a great deal more besides, he was afraid to do so. All his life he had fought to keep the strange dreams and visions at bay, but to summon them deliberately was another matter altogether. The consequences for such audacity were beyond reckoning.

Confused and uncertain, he turned to look at his

mother. In her eyes, he saw the years ahead spread out before him like a vast tapestry. There he saw the one who would join him, and with whom he would share his innermost thoughts. Arthur … Like two shooting stars they would create a light so bright it would illumine the very heavens. And through their deeds men would see what was possible within their brief lives, and would then strive to uphold the virtues of honour and courage, and to cherish the sacred depths of existence as well. He saw also that long after he and Arthur were gone there would be many who would dream of all they had accomplished, and they too would strive to attain the vision splendid.

A shiver of unease crept along the nape of Vortigern's neck to see Merlin so reluctant to speak out about the difficulties with his fort. 'By the rood, tell me what you see,' he demanded, his hand on his sword.

'The time has come, child of light, to decide where you stand,' cautioned his mother in words that were never spoken. 'Have the courage to choose the path that will benefit many.'

As Merlin looked once more at those around him, his anger and frustration began to dissolve. These were indeed dangerous times, and when it came to the hearts of men all too often they proved faint-hearted. Yet even though he doubted their ability to create a better world, he could sense their ache to know one. He saw also that there was no way for these men to progress beyond the paralysing effects of fear, unless someone showed them the way forward. This, he realised, was the path he had chosen from the first, and as difficult as this might be, he was glad of it.

In that instant the die was cast. Merlin felt the cold whip of the wind on his cheek as some part of him stood upon the distant hill of Dinas Emrys. And there in that elevated place, he saw that in spite of the solid ground, the great foundation stones of Vortigern's fort had indeed been swallowed up.

'Command your men to dig deep,' uttered Merlin in a voice he did not recognise, 'and there you shall find the pool where your squared stones now lie. At the bottom of that selfsame pool are two hollow rocks within which two mighty dragons sleep.'

Filled with sudden hope, and ignoring the disbelief of his advisers, Vortigern immediately commanded his men to take up their mattocks and shovels and dig. Not stopping when they reached the pool, they drained it outright, and there beneath the waters stood two rocks as Merlin had foretold. Then as the men struck the rocks, they were split asunder, and out of them issued two dragons, one red and one white. Then an awful battle ensued that filled all who looked on with dread. At first the white dragon seemed triumphant, but then the red dragon gained an unexpected advantage, and rising up, slaughtered the white dragon outright.

When the king asked what this might portend, Merlin became deathly pale. The vision he had held for so long now was fading and his life force was exceedingly low. As he reached out to steady himself, large beads of sweat trickled down his forehead and cheeks. Cold he was, cold as death.

'Tell me at once what this means,' demanded the king.

As Merlin fought to keep the vision before him, he could sense the fear and the envy that darkened the hearts of those around him. How they itched to dispatch him, and yet they dared not. This, he realised, was the price he would always pay if he were to have the courage to use his formidable gifts. Yet while it pierced him to the core to know this, he also knew that he had come to this world to set men free from their brutal ways. So he put aside any thought of himself and summoned what little life force remained so that he could address the king once more.

Had the words that issued forth been his own, Merlin might well have struggled how best to tell Vortigern of his dread fate, but as he opened his mouth to speak the gods took possession of him.

'Thy days are numbered,' he warned. 'This dark tower will be built as you intended, but know that the wheel of life keeps on turning. Thyself and all who dwell there will one day be consumed by fire.'

A deathly hush fell over those gathered to hear such

pronouncements, but Vortigern was strangely unmoved by these dire predictions. He knew that within Merlin he had found one with exceptional powers of Sight, who was true and without malice of any kind. And so from that day forward, Merlin was to enjoy the protection of the High King, and of those who were to rule long after Vortigern was gone.

AUTHOR'S NOTE

As Merlin foretold, Vortigern did build his hill fort on Dinas Emrys, and there he lived out his few remaining years ever fearful of those who might destroy him. Eventually, Ambrosius Aurelius and Uther Pendragon attacked his hill fort and set it alight, destroying the fortification and all who dwelt there. The years that followed were bloody. First Uther was king, then during Arthur's reign peace finally descended, for a while at least.

Looking back, it is easy to chart Merlin's destiny. Without doubt he possessed a depth of magic that the world has rarely seen. Yet because we know Merlin best as prophet and magician, we rarely give any thought to what it would have been like to be born in such dangerous times and to grow up under a cloud of contempt, without the support of parents or a mentor to nurture his extraordinary talents.

The price for Merlin's awesome gifts was high. He was destined always to be the outsider, to be the one to watch or to fear. Yet in spite of all Merlin had to endure, he and Arthur did change the world as it was known.

Like much of his life, Merlin's current whereabouts are shrouded in mystery. Some say he sailed away in a ship of glass to the Isle of Bardsey with the thirteen magical treasures of Britain. These precious objects included the veil of Arthur that made all who wore it invisible; the horn of Brangaled, which provided whatever liquor one desired; Morgan's chair, which carried whoever sat on it wherever they chose; and the whetstone of Tudno, which would only sharpen the weapons of the brave. Wherever Merlin now rests we can be sure that he guards the true throne of Britain, waiting for Arthur to return.

IN COED CELYDDON

Juliet Marillier

he forest was forbidden. Coed Celyddon was a perilous place, especially now there was a war on. Tribe fought tribe: Ector's men against Hywel's, Drustan's warriors against the Red Bull crowd from Rheged. Then there were the others, dangerous others. Pictish mercenaries had a habit of popping up when least expected, all wild tattoos and crossbows, and to the south and east was the real enemy: the Saxons.

Before he rode off to battle, Ector had given the three boys a lecture, short and sharp as always. One: keep out of trouble. Two: work hard. When these skirmishes were over, and he had that fool Hywel on his knees begging for mercy, Ector would come home and see who had improved the most at swordcraft, and archery, and riding. He liked them to compete, to challenge one another. Three: stay out of Coed Celyddon, or he'd tan their hides for them.

Cei, Ector's son, was the biggest of the three boys. He always won when size mattered, for instance in wrestling, which was not part of the official curriculum. Cei's cousin, Bedwyr, come to stay for the summer, was the smallest. Bedwyr had a talent for throwing: the spear was his favourite weapon. He might be only twelve, but grown men came out to watch him at target practice, and sometimes clapped. As for Arthur, he was in the middle: smaller than Cei, bigger than Bedwyr. Turned fourteen last midwinter day, Arthur was too young to go to battle and too old to be content with staying at home. He was good at everything, best at nothing. It came with being a foster-son, he thought: that feeling of always coming in second. He never said so, of course. Ector had been kind to him, and although Cei punched him sometimes, it was in a friendly sort of way, soon forgiven. All the same, Arthur would have liked to shine, perhaps with the sword. Not much hope of that; he didn't even have a real one of his own, only the rough practice blades the master-at-arms, Owain the Fists, gave them to work with, blunt-edged and poorly balanced. Cei had a proper sword, long and heavy, with watery patterns all along the length of it; his father had given it to him. Arthur's father never came to see him. He was away somewhere in the south, fighting battles of his own. Arthur couldn't remember what he looked like.

'Come on!' hissed Bedwyr, crouching down low as the three boys snaked their way up the hill through long grass and bracken to the shadowy edge of the woods. The dog, Cabal, padded silently behind. Ector was gone on his campaign, but there were others who might see them and call them back. Cei's mother was like a dragon, and it was not for nothing Owain the Fists had earned the nickname Ogre.

They reached the trees, slipping in under sharp-toothed holly bushes to the deeper shadow cast by great oaks. Coed Celyddon was huge, dark and mysterious: the perfect place for exploring, and all the better because it was out of bounds. Each of them was armed; they weren't stupid. Hywel's tribe had been known to slip spies in right to the fringes of Ector's land. Cei bore a bow and quiver, Bedwyr carried a throwing-spear, and Arthur had a knife in his belt.

'Right,' said Cei, assuming command in that way he had. 'Let's find this druid.'

They all knew the druid, of course. He dwelt in the heart of the forest somewhere, all alone, and came down twice a year to Ector's stronghold on the feast days of midsummer and midwinter. There were no prizes for guessing why: the fellow liked his food, and Ector always put on a good spread of roast boar, jellied eels, salmon seethed in buttermilk, pastries and fruit tarts. Strong mead flowed freely. After his third goblet, the druid could be persuaded to tell stories, wondrous tales of gods and goddesses, heroes and monsters, treachery and courage that put his audience in another world, and had them begging for more the instant he'd finished.

Afterwards, the druid sat by the fire and stared into the flames. Folk gave him a wide berth; it was common knowledge that if a druid took a dislike to you, he could turn you into a cockroach or a newt. Arthur talked to him. Arthur couldn't see the point in being afraid when it stopped him from finding out something interesting, and the druid certainly had a lot to tell. He never told his name, though. He'd say to one man it was Corr, and to another man Faol, and the next time he came he'd tell them he was called Dobhran. Those weren't proper names at all, they were animals: Crane, Wolf, Otter. Some people said the druid's real name was Myrddin or Merlin, which was disappointingly ordinary.

The druid had a knack for disappearing. One moment he'd be sitting there having a word with Arthur, and then all at once he'd be gone. He had a hideout in the woods, a place the boys had never been able to find, though they'd tried hard enough. It was as if the branches and bushes, the twisting twigs and snapping tendrils shifted about, making a net to block the way.

'I think north,' said Bedwyr. 'Under the beeches, by the pond, down the hill a bit.'

'I think south,' said Cei. 'You know where the big rock is, the one that looks like an old man with a beard? I think we should look there again.'

Arthur said nothing. He was watching his dog, Cabal. Cabal was a half-breed, part wolfhound, part something really ugly. He'd been born by mistake, and Ogre had been going to drown him. Begged politely, the master-at-arms had let Arthur keep the scrawny pup. Cabal's legs were too long for his grey, hairy body; his ears stuck obstinately upwards instead of drooping elegantly, and his long tongue perpetually hung from his grinning mouth in panting enthusiasm. Ogre had predicted Arthur would never make anything of such a misbegotten creature, but Arthur had known from the start that this was wrong. Cabal was a dog of high intelligence, and flawlessly obedient to his master. With others, he was less reliable. He'd nearly bitten Cei's finger off once.

'That way,' Arthur said as the hound, sniffing frantically, headed off down a middle path, a narrow, rough track twisting and turning into the dark heart of the wood. He went after the dog, soft-footed on the uneven ground, and the others followed him without a word.

It wasn't the easiest path. It sidled past thorny bushes, it toppled into swampy hollows and clawed its way up steep, overgrown slopes studded with unexpected rocks. They rested on a hilltop by a gushing spring. There was a view from here, over the dense, purple-green blanket of the great forest toward open heath. Cei stood balanced on a flat rock, gazing southwards: there lay the region of Cumbria, Hywel's land. Somewhere out there Cei's father was even now fighting his rival chieftain: fighting, and maybe dying. Cei wouldn't be able to see anything, though. It was too far away.

'He'll be all right,' Arthur said quietly. 'By new moon he'll be back home large as life, full of tales about brave deeds and vanquished Cumbrians, see if he isn't.'

'Of course he'll be all right!' snapped Cei, seizing his bow and heading off over the hill. 'Did you think I was worried or something? Now come on, we haven't got all day.'

It was Bedwyr's fault that they got separated. They were walking along a narrow track under low-branched beeches, single file, when he thought he saw something, a boar, a deer, and, balancing his spear with the instinct of a true hunter, ran off between the trees in hot pursuit, the dog at his heels. When Cabal came back, he was on his own. A pox on Bedwyr. It wasn't safe for both Cei and Arthur to leave the track; they might never find their way out of the forest then, judging by the tricks it had played on them in the past. They couldn't just wait, either: what if Bedwyr were hurt, gored by a tusk, pierced by an antler? They called out as hard as they could — Cabal's voice was the loudest — but the only reply was squirrels rustling in the canopy above, and the buzz of insects about their summer business.

'You go after him,' Arthur said. 'I'll wait here. If you're too long, I'll run back for help. You'd better take Cabal with you.'

There was a small clearing close by. He sat there on a fallen tree and tried to judge the time of day by the sunlight filtering down through the arch of foliage high above. He couldn't stay long; if there was something wrong, he'd need to run all the way home and get back here with Ogre or another of the men before nightfall. Only a fool would linger in Coed Celyddon after dusk.

The light changed slowly; time passed, and Arthur's head was full of unwelcome images: Bedwyr lying injured, all alone; Cei wandering lost, brambles tearing at his clothes, cobwebs blinding him, blundering deeper and deeper into the darkness of the woods. Cabal facing a savage boar, a ravenous wolf. This was no good; he had to do something, and do it now. Arthur sprang to his feet, and at that moment there was a sound of movement along the track ahead of him. Someone was coming, and fast.

'Bedwyr?' he called hopefully. But it was not his friend who ran into sight, emerging into a patch of dappled light where the sun touched the earthen path with gold. It was the hound, Cabal, tongue lolling, tail thrashing, every part of him bouncing with energy. After him came another dog, squatter, thicker, with a short, liver-brown pelt, and the very same look of mischief in his eye. The two of them raced each other across the clearing, twisting and turning, rolling in play-fight, pausing to sniff and greet a moment, and an instant later bounding about again in a kind of mad, canine dance. Arthur began to laugh: who but Cabal would find a friend in such an unlikely spot? A twig cracked. His laughter died in his throat. He drew his knife quickly and silently; Ogre had taught him well.

There was a boy on the other side of the clearing, standing half in shadow. The boy was holding a bow; the string was drawn taut, the arrow poised for flight, aimed straight at Arthur's chest. The boy was wearing a scarlet band around his head, knotted at the back. Everyone knew what that meant. He was one of Hywel's tribe: the enemy. A spy, right here in Coed Celyddon, at Ector's very doorstep.

The boy stood still as stone. His eyes were hard; his mouth was set in a thin line. He was pale as chalk. Arthur had the knife in his hand. He could throw it; it would have to be a very good shot to do any damage before that arrow reached him. Arthur had never killed a man before, only rabbits, hunting. He looked across the clearing, into the boy's narrowed eyes, and wondered how it would feel to die.

The dogs made another wild pass through the undergrowth, a mock chase ending in a complicated tumble. The two of them flopped down together on the path between the boys, breathing hard, mouths open, tongues hanging pinkly. Cabal rolled onto his back, grinning, and the other hound licked his ear.

Arthur looked at the red-scarfed boy, and the boy looked back. Very slowly, Arthur lowered the knife and sheathed it, putting out his two hands to show he carried no other weapons. For a moment he gazed straight at that arrow-point, in perfect line with his heart. He did not move. Then the boy brought down the bow, and put the arrow back in the quiver. There was nothing to say. They watched the dogs a moment; the two creatures were tired of play for now, and lay side by side in the leaf-mould, each watching his master.

'Come on, Cabal.' Arthur clicked his fingers. The other boy gave a short whistle, and the liver-coloured dog got up and went to him. Cabal stood by Arthur's side, obedient as ever. The red-scarfed boy gave a sort of nod, and Arthur nodded back. He had the strangest feeling, as if some great change had occurred, something that would make his whole life different. Were these tears in his eyes? Impossible. At midwinter he would be fifteen. He would be a man, and a man does not weep. He watched dog and boy as they vanished back under the trees, gone like shadows, gone as if they had never been, save for the disturbance of the ground made by eight scuffling hound-feet. 'Come on,' he said again. 'I think we'd better go and look for the others.'

The forest of Coed Celyddon was full of surprises. Arthur set off, expecting a long, fruitless search, followed by an uncomfortable night huddled in some chilly hollow between oak-roots. He retraced his steps, thinking to set Cabal after the others' scent, and track them as far as he could before dusk fell. But the path had changed. It was not narrow and shady any more, twisting and turning, but ran broad and straight. It did not slope downwards as before, but ran up to the top of a neat, conical hill crowned with a circle of massive oaks. From within the circle, a plume of smoke rose, and there was a smell of frying sausages. By the time Arthur reached the top, with Cabal a step behind, he was not so very surprised to see Cei and Bedwyr sitting on one side of a small, bright campfire, and on the other side, the druid squatting down to inspect the sizzling contents of the frying pan set on the coals, and muttering to himself. There was a tiny hut of stone, and a well, and a crow pecking at something underneath low twiggy bushes. The oaks stood dark and solid, like a ring of wise old folk watching and listening. Arthur stepped into the circle.

'What took you so long?' Bedwyr asked, accepting a sausage and wincing as it burned his fingers.

'We've been here ages,' said Cei. 'Where were you?'

Arthur opened his mouth to tell them, and shut it again. There was no doubt what Cei would do if he heard there was one of Hywel's tribe lurking so close to his father's stronghold. He'd be off in a flash, bow at the ready, and it would take more than a couple of dogs to stop him from shooting.

'I got lost,' Arthur said. 'Can I have one of those?'

They ate in silence; the food was too good to get less than their full attention. Whatever was in the sausages, they tasted wonderful. Of course, druids could do some strange things, so the tales went. They could probably make sausages out of thin air, if they wanted.

The meal was finished. The druid gave them water from the well; it tasted fresh and clean, like a mouthful of sunshine.

'Can you do real magic?' Bedwyr asked abruptly, as if he'd been working up to the question a while.

'Real magic?' the druid asked, raising his brows. He was not an old man; he stood tall and straight, his long plaited hair dark as night, his eyes so pale you couldn't tell what colour they really were. All the same, he had an old look, as if he'd been around as long as those oak trees had.

'You know,' said Cei eagerly. 'Changing things, and

seeing the future, that kind of magic. Can you do any?'

'Conjurer's tricks?' the druid asked in scathing tones, and an instant later, where the crow had squawked and pecked under the bushes, a black cat lay curled on itself, watching them balefully through slitted eyes. 'If that is your understanding of magic, you have much to learn. Would you see your own future? Could you gain wisdom from that?'

'Maybe,' Cei said, more hesitant now. 'I wouldn't mind a try.'

Arthur said nothing. It was odd; the druid hadn't looked at him once, and yet he felt those pale eyes following him, intent, searching, as if they could see right inside him.

Now Myrddin, if that was his name, had passed long, bony hands over the fire, once, twice, three times, and a cloud of wispy smoke, blue-tinged, arose and settled above the glowing coals.

'Look now, Cei son of Ector,' the druid said.

Cei stared into the smoke, eyes wide. Arthur couldn't see a thing, but evidently Cei could: his face changed, he frowned, then grinned, and after a while sat back on his heels, blinking.

'What did you see?' Bedwyr demanded. 'Tell us, go on!'

'A battle: I was in it, and winning,' Cei said slowly. 'A lot of blood. And later, there was …' He stopped, a violent blush rising to his cheeks.

41

'I bet Rhian the miller's daughter was in it,' Bedwyr said, laughing. 'Me next. Please.'

Afterwards, Bedwyr was less keen than Cei to say what he had seen. He'd gone very serious, and sat in silence, as if thinking hard. The future is not always as we would wish it when we are twelve years old.

'Now, Arthur,' said Myrddin. 'Do you not wish to look into the flames and see your own destiny?'

There was a lengthy silence.

'No,' Arthur said eventually. 'I don't need to. Knowing beforehand just makes it harder.'

'Makes what harder?' Cei asked, puzzled.

'Doing what's right,' said Arthur, thinking of that boy, and the arrow, and the dogs. 'Making other people do what's right. Going on when it gets difficult. All those things.' He looked up at the druid, who was regarding him gravely with those eyes that seemed to see so much. 'I want to ask you something.'

Myrddin inclined his head, waiting.

'If we stopped fighting each other, the tribes, I mean, if we made peace and helped each other instead, then couldn't we —'

'That's a stupid idea!' Cei snapped. 'Make peace with Hywel's people? They're scum, every one of them. The Red Bull tribe are a bunch of oafs, Father says so. They're our enemies.'

'All the same,' Arthur said, 'just imagine it. All the

tribes together, under one leader. What a great army that would be. A force as strong as that could beat the Saxons. An army like that could drive them out, and save our lands. We could do it. We're all the same kind underneath, Hywel's men, Ector's, Drustan's. Why shouldn't we do it?'

There was a pause.

'That's the worst idea I ever heard,' Cei said crossly. 'Us, teaming up with Cumbrians? No leader would be fool enough to try that. It's crazy!' He tossed a handful of pebbles into the fire.

'I don't know,' said Bedwyr. 'It could work. Maybe not yet, but some time. My father says —'

'What would he know?' muttered Cei.

Arthur was silent. He could see it in his head, the image bold and bright: a great, strong army, all the chieftains of Britain with their banners, a tide of courage rolling across the land, sweeping the invader before it. And when the last battle was over, a time of peace, a time for harvest and celebrations, good fellowship and wise rule. Who would lead them he did not know, but the time would come: he had never been so sure of anything.

'It's getting late,' Myrddin observed, rising to his feet. 'You'd best be off, if you don't want to risk the dragon's tongue. Now that you know how to find me, I expect to see more of you. Bring that muddle-footed hound with you. I like him.'

43

Arthur was last to go. He bowed to the druid politely. 'Thank you,' he said.

'Ah,' said Myrddin, 'don't thank me. This is your own vision, and it is for you to achieve it, not I. I'm good for a little advice from time to time, and a sausage or two. Off you go, now.'

Down the hill they went, along the track, under the beeches, over the rocks, all the way to the margin of Coed Celyddon. Of red-scarfed spy and brown-haired dog there was no sign; the only sound was the whisper of their feet in the undergrowth. First went Cei, who liked to lead. Next came Bedwyr, spear in hand, a little frown on his brow. Arthur came last, with Cabal padding beside him. Arthur's head was full of dreams. As for Cabal, being a dog, he was probably thinking of supper.

AUTHOR'S NOTE

I wanted to write a story about the real Arthur. In the oldest chronicles he was a courageous warlord who united the sixth-century tribes of Britain to keep out the invading Saxons. Coed Celyddon (the 'Scottish Wood') was the scene of one great battle. In the first tales of Arthur there's no Lancelot, no Holy Grail, not even a Round Table — writers added all those later. Still, Arthur must have been an exceptional man to have such a legend grow up around him, long after his death. The original Arthur did have two loyal friends, Cei and Bedwyr (Kay and Bedivere in the legend), and he did have a dog called Cabal. As for Myrddin, or whatever his name was, he put himself into my story without being asked.

ϻORGAN OϜ ϮHE ϜAY

Kate Forsyth

Ͽhere are those who believe that we of the fay are immortal. They are wrong. We are born, we grow, we die, just like any other living creature. It is true that time moves to a different rhythm in the realm of Annwn but that does not mean we do not know death, as the bards have sung so falsely for so long.

For only those who know they will die can be wise. I have been called many things but of them all, Morgan the Wise is, I hope, the truest.

I was fifteen when I first understood death and fifteen when I first lay with a man, clenching the seeds of his loving deep within me so that another child could sprout into life. Like the two gatehouses of a bridge spanning a turbulent river, the end of one life and the beginning of another mark my passage from child to woman, from sure innocence to uncertain knowledge. And so it is the story of my fifteenth summer that you must know, if you are to understand how I came to be who I am.

I was born Margante, eldest grand-daughter of Afallach, lord of Annwn, called by some the Fortunate Isle, for its richness and beauty; by others the Isle of Apples, for its fruit-laden orchards; and yet again, Caer Siddi or the Fairy Fortress, by those who have cause to fear the fay.

Like my home, my name changes according to the namer. Those who love me most call me Morgan, a nickname given me by my youngest sister Thitis when first she began to babble.

There were nine of us, a blessed number to those of our kind. When I was fifteen, Thitis was little more than two years old and the joy of my heart. I do not know if I loved her more at play, squealing with joy, or at night, when I carried her to bed, her downy head nestled against my shoulder. For my mother had died in the bearing of her, and so I was the only mother Thitis ever knew.

You may wonder why it was not my mother's death that first brought me face to face with mortality. You must realise my mother had born nine daughters in thirteen years. She was worn and tired, and short of temper. She had believed the tales the bards sang, of the Fortunate Isle where death and sickness were unknown, where crops grew without cultivation, and the Tylwyth Teg danced the nights away. She was human, poor thing, seduced from her own people when only a girl herself. My father Owain rode up out of the water, smiling, holding down his hand to her. She took it, laughing as he drew her up before him and galloped back into the misty waters of the lake. Of course, she regretted it afterwards but it was too late then. We of the Tylwyth Teg do not let go easily.

So although I was sorry when my mother died, my grief was not very deep nor lasting, and certainly did not make me understand the fragility of my own life. I was healthy and strong, and busy with my own concerns. For, despite what the bards sing, the gardens and orchards of Annwn do need care. Not as much as the fields of humans, of course. We of the fay do not mind dandelions and clover mingling with our corn and beans, and dislike seeing things laid out in rows and squares, as you humans labour so hard to achieve. We let the wind and the birds and the bees help us in our labour, and sing as we wander amid the flowers and the trees, and so you think what is done with love and merriment cannot be true work. But all of us have our work to do, even a princess with the blood of gods and goddesses running in her veins.

Always, too, there were my lessons. I was of the Tylwyth Teg and magic was bred in my bones. I was hungry for such knowledge and so at the age of twelve, not long before my mother died, I was given into the care of the druids, to learn what I could.

It was at the druids' school that I first met Anna, daughter of Uther Pendragon, who had been sent to the Isle of Apples to learn the seven arts. We were distant cousins of sorts, for Anna could trace her lineage back to Llyr of the Sea through her mother Igraine, and Llyr had been married to my grandfather's sister Penarddun. It may seem strange to you that eleven generations had lived and died between Penarddun and Anna, and only one between my grandfather and me, but that is the nature of time in Annwn.

Anna was a tall, fair girl, the tallest and fairest I had ever seen. Beside her I was little and dark, which at first made me hate her. No-one could hate Anna for long, though. She was like a soft white cat with round blue eyes and a satisfied purr. It did not take her long to win me over completely. She admired my grey eyes and nicknamed me Argante, and I called her Ermine for her thick pelt of pale hair.

We were as close as any sisters those three years we studied together. I must admit my lessons suffered, for we were always laughing and whispering together at the edge of the grove instead of listening to our teachers. Anna and I told each other everything in those first ardent years of our friendship and so, you see, it was my fault that her brother came raiding upon our shores.

They say I hate Arthur, son of Uther Pendragon, and indeed I have reason to. Yet did I not give him Caledfwlch, forged here upon our shores and imbued with the powers of Annwn? And when the magic of the sword was not, in the end, enough to save him, did he not know to call for me and did I not go? Would I have done so if I hated him as I should?

The stories they tell of Arthur, which you listen to with such eagerness, they are like an apple that has been baked with honey and studded with cloves, and hung from a silk ribbon. It no longer looks like an apple or smells like an apple, but cut it open and inside you will find pips. Plant these seeds and an apple tree will grow.

So here is the truth of it, the apple beneath the spices and honey. I hate Arthur for his murdering and plundering, and for the blood he spilt that day, and yet it was because of that blood that I first felt sorrow and terror and joy too, in the flame that can leap between man and woman, and in the painful tenderness that comes with the bringing forth of new life. With this knowledge, I learnt to see beyond the flimsy membrane that separates life and death. If it was not for Arthur I may never have become, in the end, Morgan the Wise.

It was a bright autumn day when Arthur's ship *Prydwen* came sailing through the mists towards our shores. Belle Garde shone upon its hill like a blue flame, its many-faceted towers glittering where the sun struck. I was playing in the garden with the youngest of my sisters, Vevan and Thitis, while Anna reclined on the grass, being far too lazy to want to toss a ball around.

Suddenly she lifted herself up, pointing. 'Look, a ship!'

We all stood staring at the boat with its high sternpost and large steering oars, its great square sail painted with some device in red. We were rather surprised, though it was not unknown for strangers to find their way through the haze of mirage that conceals our realm. In those days the doors between the worlds stood ajar and there was much traffic between those of human blood and those of the fay. The doors are all locked now, of course, and only those who have the key may open them. We of the Tylwyth Teg are not so trusting as we once were.

As I stood gazing at the ship, I felt an odd frisson down the back of my neck, as if someone had crept up behind me and blown on my skin. I shuddered and rubbed my arms, although I was not cold.

'Let's go down to the dock and see who it is,' Vevan cried. 'We aren't expecting visitors, are we, Morgan?'

I shook my head. 'Not that I know of. Surely Taidi would've let me know if he was expecting anybody?' I dusted leaves and grass from my skirt and held down my hand to Anna. 'Coming?'

'Of course,' she answered. 'Miss the one exciting thing to happen here since I got back? Let's hope it's a boatload of handsome young warriors who have lost their way. Maybe we can entice them to stay awhile?'

I smiled, though I still felt that puzzling tightening of my nerves. I was not concerned by the impact of unexpected guests on our larder, for we always had the cauldron of plenty to tide us over any need for food, nor was I worried about where to house the travellers, for my grandfather's castle was vast. I felt no fear, for what could one small ship do against the warriors of the Tylwyth Teg? It was a chill akin to fear that troubled me, however, and being still a child myself, I shrugged it away and went running down through the garden as eagerly as the others.

We were not the only ones to make our way towards the jetty, for we of the fay are always curious and eager for any diversion. Children came running and shouting down the road, men laid down their harps or set aside their tools, and women came wandering out of the forests, many of them with flowers entwined in their hair and their mouths stained red with berries. By the time the ship was dropping her sails and sliding in beside the jetty, there was a jostling crowd waiting for her, all talking and laughing.

'Look at the red dragon on her sail,' Anna cried excitedly. 'That is Arthur's device! What can he be doing here?' The animation in her face faded, and she frowned. 'It is only a month or so since I saw him. I hope nothing is wrong ...'

Then she began to wave and call, for a tall, young warrior was leaning over the bulwark. He leapt down and embraced Anna affectionately. I looked him over curiously, for I had heard a great deal about the young king. He was as big and handsome as Anna had said, his hair and beard near as fair as hers and his eyes as blue. He was not yet twenty, but he was battle-hardened and battle-scarred. He had seen heavy fighting since he won the throne, I had heard, and certainly the guilelessness of his youth had been worn away, I could see that at once.

He met my gaze with his own, bold and raking. 'So this is your beloved Argante. She is almost as beautiful as you describe, Anna, at least for a fairy. I wonder if she is as clever?'

I felt anger roaring in my ears. I cast him one disdainful glance and said, very distinctly, 'It would not be difficult to be more clever than a bone-headed warrior whose ears are still ringing from the last battle he fought.'

King Arthur laughed. He cast me a look of admiration. If I had not sensed the mockery behind it, I might have half-swooned from the warmth of it but I drew myself away, feeling again a shudder of dread. It may merely have been fear at the power such a man might have over me. I do not think so now, however. I am old enough now to recognise the chill breath of foreboding.

A small band of men alighted from the ship, among them a beautiful, slightly built man whom I recognised. This was the bard Taliesen, who had once been a peasant boy in the employ of the great seer Ceridwen. One day, stirring her cauldron, three drops of a magical potion spat out and burnt his hand. Sucking the burn, he had tasted the elixir of knowledge meant for her son and at once knew all the secrets of the universe.

Knowing Ceridwen would never forgive him, Taliesen fled. He turned into a hare, she turned into a hound. He turned into a fish, she became an otter. When he grew wings and took to the sky, she transformed into a hawk. At last, in desperation, he hid himself in the shape of a grain of wheat. Ceridwen changed into a hen and ate him.

That should have been the end of him but once Ceridwen resumed her usual shape, she found she was pregnant. In time she bore a baby boy who was so beautiful she could not bear to kill him. She trussed him up in a leather bag and threw him into the sea. Two days later he was rescued by a prince who raised the boy as his own, calling him Taliesin, which means 'Shining Brow'. He grew to be a great bard and seer, though one with little love for the fay.

At the sight of Taliesen, I fell behind, troubled and unsure. All seemed well. King Arthur and his men were looking about them with pleasure. My indolent Anna was the most animated I had ever seen. Everyone was smiling and laughing. Everyone, that is, except Taliesen the bard and I.

The doors of the castle stood open, welcoming light spilling out into the gloaming. My grandfather sat in his throne at the head of the great hall, his nine white hounds lying at his feet. They raised their heads and snarled as King Arthur came in. I was glad to see how the king's step faltered, though it was only for a moment. He ignored the growling dogs, with their ears and eyes as red as blood, and bowed low over my grandfather's hand.

I left the men to their polite fencing, and withdrew to my rooms to change for what promised to be a long and tedious night, listening to Anna's brother boast of his doings and watching her hang on his arm and believe every word. When I came down, the great hall was set up with tables and trestles, the minstrels were playing, and King Arthur sat on my grandfather's left hand, my father Owain on his right. On a side table sat the cauldron of plenty, its golden sides gleaming in the candlelight. It was one of the treasures of Annwn, made by Bran the Blessed himself. With pearls all round its rim, it could only be kindled by the breath of nine maidens. It would produce the most delicious food until all that sat at the table were replete, filled with new strength and vigour.

I saw how the eyes of all King Arthur's men dwelled on the cauldron, but even then I had no true understanding of what they planned to do. I blamed my unease on childish jealousy, and tried my best to suppress it.

My grandfather stood with some effort, for he was many centuries old now. He nodded at King Arthur and his men and raised his goblet. 'Welcome to my realm, my boy,' he said. 'We are glad to meet you at last, for we have heard how you seek to bring peace to the land after a hundred years of bloodshed. We wish you well and are glad of the chance to forge strong bonds with you, who carry the blood of Llyr in your veins, even as we do. It is good that you should know us, for other races and other gods have come and we have been afraid that the old ways would be cast aside. May the Children of Llyr and the Children of Don flourish and stand strong, and may there be peace and plenty in the land!'

Goblets were drained with enthusiasm all round the room, though I noticed the strangers did not drink, just held their cups to their lips and pretended to taste the wine within. I smiled to myself. They believed the old superstitions that to eat or drink when in the land of the fay was to be trapped in that realm forever. What were they to do once the cauldron started pouring forth its bounty?

Except that it did not. When I and my eight sisters held hands and blew gently upon the cauldron, the water within barely trembled. A mutter of shock and consternation rose all round the room.

King Arthur turned on his sister. 'Are all your tales of the cauldron of Annwn nothing but lies?' he hissed. 'We have come all this way for a fairytale?'

'There is a coward among us!' my father cried at the same moment. 'The cauldron will not feed the craven.'

'Or the treacherous,' my grandfather said softly. He had heard King Arthur's furious words, even if my father had not. 'You think I did not notice that you refused to drink my toast? Even such fools as men hesitate to break the law of hospitality. You plan to steal my cauldron? And plunder the riches of my land? Is that the truth of it?'

'No, no!' Anna cried. 'Arthur, you wouldn't ...' She cast a glance at me and I saw at once that she had been the one to tell him of our treasure, the cauldron that could feed and succour an army. I glared at her in sudden, bitter hatred.

My father had leapt to his feet, catching up his

eating knife in one hand. 'Treachery! You come with foul intent! The cauldron will not serve those with such base ambitions,' he cried. He was always impulsive, my father, quick to word and blow. He lunged at King Arthur with his dagger, who dodged nimbly, seizing his own knife. There was a quick weave and duck and flurry of blows, and suddenly my father cried out and slumped to the floor. His blood sprayed across my face.

Trestles crashed against the flagstones as men leapt to their feet. All was confusion. My sisters screamed. I fell to my knees, cradling my father's head. His hair was sticky with blood. My grandfather bellowed and raised his walking stick, lashing King Arthur across the back. He stumbled with a cry, and one of his men struck my grandfather deep in the breast. He fell stiffly, his eyes wide open in shock. His head hit the stone with a clunk. I sat silent, my ears filled with a rushing sound.

All round me men fought, with knife and chair leg and poker and platter. Then Taliesen pulled a horn from his belt and blew it. The sound rang out above the clamour and at once I knew for whom he called. That little ship, bobbing at our jetty. Many warriors must be hidden there. I tried to get to my feet, calling to my grandfather's men. My men now. No-one heeded me. I struggled to find a way through the heaving, struggling mass, but received such a blow to my head I fell to my knees. That was when Thitis, my dear sweet baby, shrieked and rushed for me.

I swear he did not mean to do it. Even in the horror of that moment, as I saw his blade swing back, its sharp tip slashing across her throat, I swear his shock and grief were as great as mine. For a moment our glances struck across her tiny, trampled body. Perhaps that is why I cannot hate him, for I saw his face at that moment and knew that he felt the stretching of time and space to very breaking point, just as I did.

I reached for her, gathered her into my arms, felt her head loll back, lifeless. The pain that struck into my chest was so acute it was as if a spear had caught me there. I was struck mute and paralysed. All around me men and fay died, but I could not hear, or see, or move. When my grief came it was as rage, a rage so dreadful flame burst from my hands and cleared a path before me. So I came into my powers, with the blood of Thitis blurring my vision and the shrieks of the dying in my ears.

We prevailed in the end. Of the hundred and fifty men who had crouched in *Prydwen*'s bilge beside their boy-king, only seven men survived, Taliesen the bard among them. We lost three hundred and seventy-three, and our king, and the king's heir, and my innocence. It was a high cost to pay.

I could have had him executed. I could have fed his entrails to my hounds. Instead, I put my mouth to his

59

wound and sucked out his blood. As he recoiled from me, I went out into the cold starry night and lay down in the embrace of the oak tree's roots. I slept, I think, a little. My mind wandered in and out of dreams. I flew with a black-winged bird over the shadowed landscape of the future, I listened to the raven's cry. When I woke in the morning, I knew many things I had not known before. I rose and washed myself clean, and spat the brown dust of his blood from my mouth. I dressed myself as a queen of the fay, and I took from the armoury a sword that had been forged by Gofannon himself, son of Don and master-smith. It too was one of the treasures of Annwn. I took it to him. He was pale, bruised and shaken in his dark cell. He stood up when I came in and faced me with as much of his usual arrogance as he could muster, though he could not help the black dilation of his eyes at the sight of the heavy sword in my hands.

For a moment we faced each other. I stood no higher than his shoulder but I was at least as proud and in no way as frightened. Then slowly I offered him the hilt of the sword.

He took it wonderingly, unable to speak.

'I have seen what is to be,' I said. 'You will need the sword. It is named Caledfwlch. Its blade shall never fail you and its sheath protects you from harm. Go from here and do not return. I shall not be so merciful again.'

'But why?' he stammered.

I took a while to answer. I would not let him see the heaviness of my grief, which lodged in my throat like a stone. 'The tide is on the turn,' I managed at last. 'The evil of the future that contains you alive is far less than the evil of a future with you dead. Though I wish I could tear out your heart for the gods you have abandoned, I know you …' I had to struggle for breath, '… I know you are the only one. Take your sword, take your ship and your sister and leave my realm. Know that it is death for you to sail here again.'

But even as I said these words I felt the chill of foreboding down my spine and knew that I lied. I did not tell him so, however, and so he took the sword and for another twenty years or more, he fought and triumphed with it.

But that is a tale for another telling. I have spoken here of death and the tasting of blood, but now it is time to show the bright face of the moon, the story of loving and the making of life. For I saw many things that night I lay in the grove with Arthur's blood in my mouth. I saw it was time to close the doors between the worlds, else all the things of magic would be lost and broken in the times of change and upheaval that beset us. I saw it was time for me to lay aside my childhood and become a woman and a queen.

So when the ashes of the dead had at last blown away on the wind, I set out with my nine hounds and

I went to a place that I knew, where a road of the humans fords the River Alun in the shadow of the Mountain of the Mothers. Such places are often doorways into our world, and so I crossed the threshold and came out into the world of men. I undid my hair, removed all my clothes and sat on a stone, washing myself in the river while my hounds howled about me.

Soon a man came riding along, as I had known he would. This man was Urien Rheged, and though he was not as young and strong as Arthur, he was lusty enough.

When he saw me, dressed only in my long black hair, he sent away all his men and came to me with long, heavy strides and seized me in his hot hands.

'What are you, witch-woman?' he said against my neck.

I said, 'I am Margante, daughter to the King of Annwn, who is now dead. God's blessing on the feet which brought you here.'

'Why?' he asked, and kissed me.

I had not expected his kiss to fire me, and so when I finally answered it was rather unsteadily. 'I am fated to wash here until I should conceive a son by a Christian man.'

He laughed and said, 'It is far too cold to sit here bathing day after day. Let me see what I can do to help you.'

And so there in the bracken, my son Owain and my daughter Morwyn were concieved, if not in love, at least in eagerness and pleasure. A year later Urien came back to the Ford of Barking and took away my twin babes, that they may be raised in the way of men. This too was a bitter grief to me, and another resentment to store up against Arthur. For I loved my children and would have given much to keep them safe with me behind the locked doors of Annwn.

I knew, though, that the world of humans needed them. Owain and Morwyn carried with them all the gifts of healing, song and merriment that I could give them, as well as the more troubling gift of foresight. In time Owain would fall in love, betray that love, run mad in the forest and befriend a lion, but all of that is yet another tale. It is enough that you know he learnt in the end that love is more important than valour, peace more important than war. For we of the Tylwyth Teg see time differently from you short-lived humans. In the small, black pip of an apple, we see the tree that will eventually flower and bear fruit.

Author's Note

Morgan le Fay is one of the most intriguing and ambivalent figures in Arthurian mythology. She is portrayed as evil sorceress, beautiful seductress, wise healer, queen, priestess, mother, wife, crone. The many echoes of her name show her many diverse manifestations: in Brittany, *morgen* means mermaid; the mirages in the Straits of Messina are known as *la fata morgana*; she is also connected with the Irish war-goddess Morrigan and with Modron, the triple-faced mother goddess of the Celts.

Morgan le Fay first appears in Geoffrey of Monmouth's *Vita Merlini* (1149) as the ruler of Avalon, a skilled healer and shape-shifter. She is identified as Arthur's sister in Chrétien de Troyes' poem 'Erec et Enide' (*c.* 1168), where she is also described as Morgan la Fee, mistress to Guigomar, Lord of Avalon. In Chrétien's poem 'Yvain' she appears as Morgan the Wise.

In Layamon's *Brut* (*c.* 1189), the first English-language rendering of Geoffrey's *Historia*, she appears as Argante the elf-queen, when the mortally wounded Arthur says, 'And I will fare to Avalun, to the fairest of all maidens, Argante the queen, an elf most fair, and she shall make my wounds all sound; make me whole with healing draughts. And afterwards I will come again to my kingdom and dwell with the Britons with mickle joy.'

Giraldus Cambrensis, in his *Speculum Ecclesia* (*c.* 1216) says 'after the battle of Camlann, the body of Arthur, who had been mortally wounded, was carried off by a certain noble matron called Morgan, who was his cousin, to the Isle of Avalon'. He also describes her as 'a certain fairy goddess … called Morganis'.

It is not until the Cistercian Vulgate Cycle (1220) that Morgan le Fay is stripped of her otherworldly origins and begins to assume the cruel, sinister and incestuous form that we now know best today.

I am most interested in the early tales of Arthur, which are found in their purest forms in the old Welsh tales. The most famous of these Welsh sources is the collection of eleven stories known as *The Mabinogion*, but there are others, including the Welsh text *Brut y Brenhinedd* (Chronicle of the Kings), which some say is the original text translated by Geoffrey of Monmouth as his *Historia Regum Britanniae* in 1136.

In particular I have drawn upon 'The Spoils of Annwn', a poem in *The Book of Taliesen*, which describes King Arthur's thwarted plan to carry off the magical cauldron of Annwn. The story of the Ford of Barking is found in a number of Welsh folktales, as well as in the thirteenth-century *Suite du Merlin*, which Malory drew upon for his *Morte d'Arthur*. I owe my greatest debt to Steve Blake and Scott Lloyd's book, *The Road to Avalon: The True Location of Arthur's Kingdom Revealed*, which examines the early Welsh material in great detail.

GAWAIN AND THE
SELKIE'S DAUGHTER

Janeen Webb

igh on a rocky headland a solitary figure stood, still and silent, outlined against a pale summer sky. His cloak stirred in the light onshore breeze, moulding itself against the bulky curves of a great bear of a man, a powerful, unmoving man in a lonely landscape of stone and sea. The man stared at the shallows of a little cove, where a group of shining seals played in the dappled sunlight, slipping and diving and sliding sleek through the green water, popping up to sun themselves on warm smooth rocks, barking softly with pleasure.

The crunching sound of footsteps on loose shingle

rose from below. A tall, well-muscled youth strode down the beach, a plaid blanket slung over his broad shoulder, a basket carried lightly on his arm. The breeze lifted his golden hair gently, and he laughed for the simple joy of being young and strong and alive. He laid his plaid carefully on a patch of dry soft sand above the damp of the sea wrack, then stripped off his clothes and folded them neatly beside the basket. Naked in the sunlight, he walked straight toward the lapping water and waded out a little way, close to a flat ledge of rock.

The watcher on the cliff top looked down intently as the largest of the seals swam away from the group, making for where the young man stood. It slid easily onto the warm rock platform, where it began at once to undulate in a curiously sinuous rippling motion.

The young man was waiting. Wordlessly, he reached down, and helped his lover step gracefully out of her sealskin.

They kissed as the pelt slid away, the young man's golden hair tangling with the dark honey of her long tresses. His skin was fair, lightly freckled in the manner of Orkney men, but hers was as white as any pearl, smooth and untouched by wind or rain or sun. Tall she was, and lithe, her breasts showing high and firm as she pressed against him, her limbs long and clean as she held him to her. And when, at last, the two drew apart, gasping and smiling, the young man picked up the sealskin and the couple splashed ashore. Gently, almost reverently, he helped his lady drape her pelt to dry on a smooth rock high above the waterline. Then he took her by her white hand and led her, unresisting, to where the old plaid rug lay warming in the sunlight for their delight.

High on the crag, King Lot allowed himself a little grunt of weary affirmation. He folded his massive arms across his chest, and his mottled face grew almost as red as his tangled auburn beard as he watched his son lay himself down in love with the selkie girl. Lot could see from the easy urgency of their meeting that this was not their first encounter.

He was determined that it would be their last.

The shadows had lengthened and the sea wind had turned chill by the time Gawain returned home, walking carefully along the narrow path that ran the length of the cliff beside the high salt-blackened stone walls of the castle. His brother Gareth was waiting for him, leaning casually against the heavy brass-studded oak gates that would soon swing shut against the night.

'You're in trouble,' said Gareth cheerfully.

'Why?'

'You know why.' Gareth smirked.

Gawain was losing patience. 'I'm not that late,' he said, guessing. 'The gates aren't shut yet.'

'It's not about being late.' Gareth paused significantly. 'Everyone knows how you sneak out at night. To visit a certain *lady*.'

Gawain grinned at his brother. 'Mind your own business.'

'I would, except the whole castle's buzzing with the news of your latest conquest.' Gareth lowered his voice. 'This is serious, brother. I slipped out to warn you. Father saw you, on the beach, with a selkie. And he's furious.'

'Oh.' Gawain paused uncomfortably. 'But what's it to him? He doesn't usually make a fuss about that sort of thing.'

'That sort of thing doesn't usually involve the seal folk,' Gareth replied darkly. 'Father has been striding about the great hall all afternoon, muttering about how you've gone too far this time. Mother has been trying to calm him down. I thought I'd better tell you. Forewarned is forearmed, as they say.'

'Thanks,' said Gawain. He dragged his fingers through his salt-stiff hair, then straightened his shoulders and strode to meet his father in the great hall of Orkney.

Lot and Morgana sat by the hearth in high, carved chairs. A tray bearing sweetmeats, a curved flagon and wine goblets was set on a low table beside them. The food was untouched. The king and queen were talking in hushed, urgent voices. The queen looked up at the sound of her son's approach, but Lot leapt to his feet.

'It's about time, my lad,' the king bellowed. 'I've been waiting for you.'

'So I see,' said Gawain. 'Is something amiss?'

'I saw you today,' the king said heavily. 'I saw what you did. Saw it with my own two eyes. You and that selkie girl. Don't try to deny it.'

'I wouldn't dream of it, Father,' Gawain replied. 'What's the problem?'

'What's the problem?' King Lot was getting red-faced. 'It won't do,' he boomed. 'My son, with a selkie! A shape-changer! I won't have it.'

'It's not for you to decide.'

'This is my kingdom. My word is law here,' the king shouted. 'And while you are under my roof, it is for me to decide.'

'Enough!' Morgana's word cracked like a whip. She stood up, tall and graceful, her long red hair glinting in the firelight. She moved deftly to stand between father and son. 'Stop it, both of you,' she said. 'This is getting us nowhere.'

The two men were momentarily silent, glaring at each other.

'We do have a problem here,' she continued smoothly. 'And we will resolve it quietly and calmly. Agreed?'

Lot spoke first. 'Agreed. Your mother is, as always, in the right of it. My hand.' He held out his huge sword-callused hand to his son.

Gawain shook his father's hand. 'Agreed.'

'Good,' said Morgana. She resumed her seat by the fire. 'So tell me, Gawain,' she said quietly, 'how it was that you came to meet a selkie girl at all.'

'It was at full moon last,' her son replied. 'I was walking along the shingle, coming back ...' He faltered.

'From the fishing village, and from the bed of that pretty little dark-eyed lass who caught your fancy,' King Lot finished for him.

Gawain looked down, shifting uncomfortably from foot to foot.

'No need to look so surprised, son,' Lot went on. 'I keep a sharp eye on my kingdom. And I paid off her father in good red gold not two weeks since. He's an understanding man where there's profit to be had. So that's settled.'

'Then why ...?'

'Why interfere now with your love-life?' King Lot snorted in disgust. 'Because today you were meddling where you should not, and no good will come of it! That's why.'

'Lot, please.' Morgana put a warning hand on her husband's arm. 'Let our son speak.' She turned her gaze back to Gawain. 'You met her by moonlight, you were saying?'

'Yes, Mother,' Gawain said simply. 'I was walking home along the beach, and she was dancing all alone on the shore.' He could not help smiling at the memory of it. 'I've never seen anything so beautiful,' he said softly. 'Naked she was, and shimmering. She looked as lovely as a goddess, all shining silver.'

Morgana quickly made the sign to avert evil. 'Be careful what you invoke,' she said swiftly. 'Even here, with me to ward you, be careful.'

'Sorry,' said Gawain. 'I never meant …'

'I know,' said his mother. 'Now tell me: did you hear music?'

Gawain thought for a moment. 'I think there was music,' he said slowly. 'Singing. But I couldn't make out the tune. It was far away, out to sea maybe. As if it was meant just for her, for her pleasure.'

'And then what happened?'

'She saw me. She opened her arms wide, and beckoned to me to join her.'

'And you were drawn to her?'

'As if I'd waited all my life for her,' Gawain said simply.

Morgana looked grave. 'Enchantment,' she said softly.

King Lot groaned. 'That's all we need,' he said. 'Morgana, this is your domain. Now what do we do?'

'We?' said Gawain quickly. 'I told you. I won't give her up. Not for anything.'

'You will have to, my dear,' Morgana said calmly.

'Before you are completely under her control.' She reached out and patted his hand. 'I command some power, but I cannot yet know if it will be enough to break the spell that binds you to her.'

Gawain pulled away abruptly. 'Isn't anyone listening to me? I don't want you to break the spell, if that's what it is. I love her. I'll marry her. I'm fifteen, I'm old enough,' he said defiantly. 'And it's not as if she isn't a suitable match. Her lineage is every bit as good as mine.'

Lot's shoulders sagged. He looked suddenly afraid. 'Gawain, are you saying what I think you're saying?'

'Only that her father is the Great Selkie. The king of all the ocean realm.' Gawain couldn't keep the note of pride and triumph from his voice.

'And all is well while he keeps to his kingdom and I to mine.'

'Then you'll have an alliance, won't you?' said Gawain.

'Don't be a fool,' said his father. 'There's always more to it than that. Does her father know?'

'I doubt it,' said Morgana. 'The sea has been calm of late.'

'We were going to tell him, to tell all of you,' said Gawain.

'When?' said Lot. 'When she's already pregnant?'

'That's it!' said Morgana. 'I should have seen it sooner.'

'Seen what?' said Gawain.

'Think,' said Morgana. She spoke slowly. 'Your great strength comes from sunlight and solid earth. Yet you are drawn to love a creature of moonlight and water, a creature of the shadowy sea. Think what might come of it.'

Gawain and his father exchanged puzzled looks.

Morgana pressed on. 'Fire, earth, air, water — all the elements together,' she said. 'Think what such a child could be, could become.'

'Oh,' said Gawain. 'I see.'

'I don't think you do,' said his mother. 'There is magic at work here, and I fear for both you and the girl. She may not have willed this union.' She paused, thinking. 'The question is, who has cast this spell, and why.'

'The question,' said Lot, 'is what's to be done about it. And I think that our first plan is still the best. The boy must make the journey to his uncle, at Camelot.'

'You can't just send me away,' said Gawain. 'I'm not a child.'

'Obviously not,' said Lot. 'That's why you have to go.'

'Peace, Lot,' said Morgana. She turned gravely to her son. 'You would have gone sooner or later to Arthur's court. It is your destiny. My brother will welcome you, and you will become the greatest of his knights.'

'Listen to your mother,' said Lot, his voice unexpectedly gruff. 'She has the second sight. We have long known that this hour would come, though we did not guess the manner of its coming.'

'Your fate is upon you,' said Morgana, 'and you must act.'

'You've learned all of sword-craft and the knightly skills that we can teach you here,' said Lot. 'And we had planned that you should go to Arthur at your sixteenth year. Orkney is too small a place for you, for what you will be. We're bringing the plan forward a little, that's all.'

'And you expect me to just leave the woman I love,' said Gawain. 'On your say-so?'

'She's no woman, son,' said Lot. 'That's the problem.'

'You cannot hold a selkie for long, my dear,' Morgana said gently. 'Even if you hide her sealskin, as some have done, she will find a way of returning to the sea. She must. It is her nature. They are shape-changers, Gawain, and they do not love as we mortals do. They cannot.'

Gawain sat down heavily in the chair opposite his mother. 'But I love her,' he said wearily.

Morgana poured wine into one of the goblets and handed it to her son. 'I know you do, dear,' she said. 'But this is enchantment, not a love freely chosen. And you cannot understand until you are free of it. I know. You will have to trust me in this.'

Gawain looked down and swirled the wine in his

goblet. 'Very well, Mother,' he said, sipping his drink. He would not meet her eyes. 'When do I leave?'

'First thing in the morning,' said Lot briskly.

Gawain drained his goblet, and stood up. 'Then I'll go straight to my chamber,' he said. 'I'll have to pack.'

'I'll send someone to help you,' said Morgana.

'Don't bother,' said Gawain. 'I need to be alone.'

'As you wish,' said the king.

'Goodnight, Mother.' Gawain kissed his mother on the cheek, nodded to his father, and strode from the hall.

'Gareth!' said Lot. 'You can come out now. I know where you're lurking!'

Gareth stepped from behind a long tapestry. 'I'm sorry, Father,' he said. 'I just wanted —'

'I know what you wanted,' said the king. 'But now I have a task for you. I need you to stay with your brother tonight. He won't welcome it, but I don't want him slipping out to call to the selkies. Do you understand?'

'Yes, Father.'

'Good. Then be off with you.'

Gareth turned to leave.

'And don't forget to kiss your lady mother goodnight.'

'Sorry.' Gareth pecked the cheek Morgana offered. 'Goodnight, Mother,' he said.

'Goodnight, Gareth,' she replied. 'And don't fret: you too will go to Camelot, in your turn.'

Gareth's face lit up with a huge smile. 'Really?'

'Really.'

Gareth left the hall, racing to catch up with his brother to tell him the news.

'That was too easily done,' said Lot. 'Gawain plans to flee. I know it.'

'Gawain will not leave the castle tonight,' said Morgana softly. 'He will sleep.' She put the stopper back firmly in the neck of the flagon, and patted a little silver vial that hung from her belt.

'What did you put in his wine?' asked Lot.

'Nothing more than an elixir of herbs,' she replied. 'He needs to rest.'

'And we have no need for him to warn the selkie girl.' The king smiled at his wife.

'Exactly,' said Morgana. 'And now, my lord, we have much to prepare if all is to be ready for Gawain's departure.'

'Aye,' said Lot. 'And we'd best get on with it.'

The queen rose, and took her husband's arm. The two left the hall together, deep in conversation.

Clear sunlight streaming through the chamber window awoke Gawain. He yawned and stretched and flung back the coverlets as usual, but before his feet had touched the floor he noticed his brother, still asleep, on a pallet that blocked the doorway. Memories of the night before came flooding back, and Gawain scowled, his sunny mood turning black in the space of a moment. He stood, took three paces across the room, and kicked Gareth, hard.

'Get up,' he shouted. 'What are you doing here? Are you supposed to be my warden, or are you just a spy? You won't stop me, you know.'

'Ouch!' said Gareth, instantly awake. 'That hurt.'

'Not as much as it hurts to be betrayed by a brother,' Gawain replied.

Gareth rubbed his injured ribs. 'I was taking care of you,' he said. 'Father made me promise.'

Gawain ignored him. 'They tricked me,' he said bitterly.

'It was for your own good,' Gareth replied. 'So you wouldn't run away to the selkies.' He stood, still massaging his ribs. 'And you *were* planning to go in the night, weren't you?'

Gawain turned away and stood at his window, looking out to sea. 'You don't understand,' he said. 'You can't.'

'I'm not completely stupid,' said Gareth. 'I know you want to be with the selkie girl. But Mother says you are enchanted. And she should know.'

King Lot strode into the chamber, cutting off further conversation. 'Well, son,' he said. 'Your men are waiting, and impatient to be off. Why aren't you dressed? Is your baggage ready?'

Gawain sighed. 'As ready as it will ever be,' he said. 'Give me a moment to dress, and I'll be ready too.'

'Good. I'll wait outside.'

There was nothing for it. Gawain splashed his face with water, and struggled into his travelling clothes. It was not long before he was stomping down the stairs to the courtyard, where a dozen armed men were already assembled.

Morgana and Lot were standing by the great hall. Gawain crossed to meet them, striding across the stones with long steps. He bent to kiss his mother's cheek, observing the formalities.

She reached out and caught his hand. 'Gawain,' she said, 'you must not part from us in anger. I know your heart is full, but we act only for the best. Destiny can be a hard master, but obey it we must.' She stretched up and kissed him. 'Go safely, my son,' she said. 'I will ward you as best I may.'

'Thank you, Mother,' said Gawain, touched despite himself.

'And I, too, bid you farewell,' said Lot gruffly. 'Make me proud, boy. I expect you to greet me as a knight when next I come to Arthur's court.'

'And so I shall, Father,' Gawain replied.

He turned away, to where Gareth waited, holding the reins of Gawain's horse. The brothers hugged briefly before Gawain swung up into his saddle. 'Farewell, brother,' he said.

'I'll be joining you soon,' Gareth replied. 'Farewell.'

Lot gave the signal, and his men clattered out of the courtyard, Gawain in the centre of the troop.

'Will he be safe?' Lot asked Morgana.

'Safe enough on land,' she replied. 'Let us hope he makes the sea crossing before the Great Selkie learns the truth of this dalliance from his daughter.'

The king's men rode briskly in the sunlight, arriving in good time at Orkney's little seaport. Gawain searched the horizon as he boarded the ship that would carry him far from home, but nothing broke the surface of the sparkling blue sea. Of the selkies there was no sign. His heart ached, knowing that his lover was waiting for him in their usual place, waiting and wondering, unaware she was betrayed.

The wind set fair as the ship sailed into the open ocean. The two guards who were to travel with Gawain to Arthur's court smiled for the simple pleasure of the breeze in their hair and the sun on their faces, and even Gawain's spirits lifted as his ship slipped smoothly over the shining water.

Land was in sight once more and the soft summer evening light had begun to fade from the sky when the weather suddenly changed, blowing up foul and treacherous. The ship pitched and rolled, and before the sailors could clamber aloft there came a squall so fast and strong that the sails snapped and tore, leaving shreds of canvas flapping about the mast.

The skies grew dark, and darker yet as great thunderclouds massed overhead, and the seas rose higher, mountains of green water sliding and rolling against each other as the huge wind whipped them about. Forked lightning split the louring sky and gigantic waves roared furiously as they crashed down upon the stricken ship. Men clung to the rigging, holding on for dear life as the ship bucked and plunged beneath them. The captain lashed himself to the kicking wheel, fighting to hold the ship out to sea, where she might run before the storm. Gawain made to help him but was caught by a monstrous breaker that washed him sideways in a swirling flood of salt water and broken rigging. He grasped anything he could, tumbling until he reached the mast, where he stood, bruised and spluttering and half-drowned, up to his waist in icy water. The gale shrieked in the rigging as the next wave struck, crashing onto the deck with a noise like thunder. Gawain watched in horror as the captain's rope snapped. The wheel spun free, and the ship slewed about. Gawain looked wildly about him and realised that the ship was already in the bay. He could see white fringes of breakers on either side. Then the vessel lurched sideways once more, and he understood, in terror, that although they were lying head to sea, they were moving backwards. With every wave that struck the ship, they were being sucked closer to certain wreck on the shore.

'Stay with the ship!' a voice shouted. 'It's our best chance!'

Gawain looked behind him. The captain was clinging to the broken and splintered wood that once housed the wheel.

'We will founder on the shore,' the captain yelled. 'And then it's every man for himself. You must swim for your lives.'

Gawain looked in disbelief at the stretch of broken water torn by rips and undertows that lay now between the ship and the safety of the beach.

'We'll try to turn,' the captain bellowed at Gawain. 'It's best if we run headlong onto the beach through the breakers.'

With all his strength Gawain held the wheel against the pounding of the sea. Slowly, the torn sails shrieking their protest in the broken rigging, the ship turned. And as it turned, the waves caught it broadside, rolling it almost onto its beam ends. But at last the vessel wallowed upright, decks awash, its prow pointing towards the shore.

Gawain braced himself for the next onslaught. He could hear nothing now above the crash and boom of the surf and the howling of the wind and the awful grinding roar of the undertow sucking pebbles down from the beach. And then another giant wave struck the struggling ship with a force that tore the wheel from Gawain's grip. The ship was lifted and flung hard upon the shore with a fearful shock that shattered the decks. The crashing of splitting timber was loud in Gawain's ears as he hauled himself upright on the side nearest the shore. He looked down at the racing, seething water, a sluice of white foam and tumbling rocks that separated him from safety.

A huge roaring sound behind him announced the next wave, and again he was drenched in icy water. He readied himself as the seething water sucked away from the beach. Then he jumped. He landed heavily in turning shingle and tried to force his way up the beach. Behind him came an awful thunder, and he knew that the next monstrous wave was at his heels.

The wall of water swept him off his feet and flung him far up the beach. His eyes and mouth and nose were full of sand. He tumbled over and over, pummelled on pebbles as the undertow dragged him back out to sea. He tried to strike out for the surface, but the sea held him down. His lungs were burning with effort. He struck out again, only to be rolled further along the ocean floor. His vision blurred with spots of bright light. His lungs filled with cold salt water and stinging sand.

And suddenly she was there. Gawain felt warm fur beneath him and he reached for her, clinging to the selkie as her strong seal body bore him swiftly to the surface. He came up spluttering and gasping, as she held his head above the boiling foam. The pounding roar of the storm was loud in his ears as she carried him shorewards with a courage and grace that astonished the boy. Then, with one last tremendous effort, she flung him high above the line of the breaking waves.

He lay still for some moments but soon righted himself, spluttering and coughing. He sat up and stared out at the boiling sea. The selkie girl had not come ashore and Gawain could make out a sleek head bobbing just beyond the line of the breakers.

'My love,' he whispered, his throat too raw for shouting. He knew she could not hear him.

'Remember me,' he heard her call. And then she dived beneath the waves and was gone.

Gawain was not alone on the beach for long. Fishermen had gathered there, risking their own lives to help the shipwrecked sailors through the pounding surf, and looking, Gawain realised, for whatever booty might come their way.

They had built a fire, and there was a warm blanket and hot broth waiting for the king's son. Gawain accepted their help in sad silence, knowing, in his heart, that the wrath of the Great Selkie had sent many of his shipmates to a watery grave.

The next morning dawned clear and bright. The sea was calm, quiet after its fury of yestereve. There was bustle in the makeshift camp as the survivors searched the shore for whatever the sea had left them. The fisherfolk would stay awhile, to bury the dead and see to the wreck. But Gawain did not tarry. He used his father's silver to hire a horse, and by midmorning he had sought directions and made his farewells.

As he crested the cliff above the cove he paused, scanning the sea one last time for his selkie love. But he saw nothing save the sparkle of sunlight on water, and heard nothing but the sighing of waves on the shore. Gawain settled himself in the saddle and turned away from the sea. He would not look back again as he rode on to Camelot.

AUTHOR'S NOTE

Sir Gawain is one of the most famous knights of the Arthurian tradition, yet also one of the most mysterious. He is nephew to King Arthur, by his sister Morgana, who is married to Lot, King of Orkney. Gawain's brothers are Agravain, Gaharet and Gareth.

Gawain has had a mixed literary history. He appears in many versions of the Arthurian tales, where he is usually described as a knight of gallantry, courtesy, and prowess. Early storytellers hailed him as the greatest of all Arthur's warriors, while later chroniclers such as Malory placed more recent heroes such as Lancelot before him. But no matter which account we choose, Gawain is always there as a great fighter, and a famous lover. What fascinates me most is that he constantly appears as a champion of women, especially where magic is involved, as it is in his celebrated encounters with women such as Lady Ragnell and Dame Bercilak.

Gawain is the quintessential 'lady's man', so it seemed fitting that a story of his youth should include a magical woman. And who could be more mysterious and enticing to the young Gawain than a selkie girl?

THE CALL OF CAMELOT

Sally Odgers

Gareth, Prince of Orkney, was three when King Lot died. Gareth had hardly known his father, and he didn't really understand what was happening. His mother, Morgawse, seemed angry, but that was normal. Queen Morgawse was no soft mother to her elder sons, although she was sometimes kind to Gareth.

'You are my boy,' she would say, fiercely stroking his hair. 'Blood of my blood, bone of my bone.' And then she would push him away.

Trying to love Morgawse was rather like trying to love a large and unpredictable dog, or the sea that lapped the shores of Orkney. A wrong move might bring a painful snap or a stinging splash of cold salt water.

Gareth admired his elder brothers, especially Gawain, who was the eldest. Gawain and slow-spoken Gaheris went around together, with cranky Agravaine tagging along. Sometimes it seemed that they didn't know Gareth existed.

Perhaps because he spent so much time in the nursery with old Nessie, Gareth was always pale and spindly. Nessie noticed this, and began to take Gareth out for rambles along the path above the shore. Sometimes Gareth looked longingly at the great pillars of rock standing out in the sea, and sometimes he watched the seals come swimming in. He ached to stroke a seal, but Nessie said no.

When Gareth was five, Morgawse left the islands for a while.

'Where are you going, my lady?' asked Gareth as she cloaked herself for the journey.

Morgawse drew him onto her knee. 'I am off to Camelot, child, to take a gift to my brother. I shall get one in return, I hope.'

'Oh.' Gareth was puzzled, as much by the twist of his mother's mouth as by the words. He liked *his* brothers. 'Is your brother big, like Gawain?'

Morgawse shrugged. 'Young Arthur Pendragon thinks himself big enough. Him with his high ideals and his knightly ways. Him in his lofty many-tower'd Camelot.'

Gareth liked the sound of that. 'Many-tower'd,' he murmured to himself. 'And what will you take him as a gift, my lady?'

'Myself.' Morgawse laughed harshly. 'I'll take him myself, and give him myself. I'll get and give a gift to make him wish he'd never been born …'

Nessie tugged at Gareth's hand. 'Come, my lamb. It's time we went for our walk.'

'What did my lady mean?' asked Gareth, as they trudged along the moorland path. The heather was in bloom, and Gareth had already picked a fistful of pink sea thrift and blue sea squill. He left the tiny primrose he found; it looked too delicate to pick.

'Foolish nonsense,' said Nessie. 'My lady is soured with revenge. Mark my words, my lamb, no good will come of it.'

'I might go to many-tower'd Camelot one day?' suggested Gareth. 'And see my lady's brother?'

Nessie clicked her tongue. 'You will not, my lamb. Foreign kingdoms are no place for a Prince of Orkney.'

'Not even Gawain?'

'As for Gawain, Gaheris and Agravaine, they'll just please themselves.' Nessie snorted. 'Those laddies always do. Not like you, my lamb. You like to please old Nessie, don't you?'

Gareth smiled, and flung out his arms. 'I like to

please *everyone*, Nessie. Specially Gawain.' He turned and looked longingly out to sea, where his mother's craft would soon be sailing. 'May we go down to look at the seals today?'

'No, laddie. Best you stay safe on dry land. You'd not like to see the selkies take old Nessie, would you?'

Gareth had heard of the strange seal-people in tales. It seemed reasonable to him that they might want Nessie. He couldn't imagine anyone not wanting Nessie. 'But I would give the selkie ladies my flowers, and then they'd not take you. So may we go?'

'Not today,' said Nessie.

Morgawse came back from Camelot with a haggard look of triumph. She seemed more distracted than ever, but when Gareth asked Nessie what was wrong, his nurse just shook her head. Then, after some months, he heard screaming from his mother's quarters. 'Nessie! Nessie! Come quickly! Someone is hurting my lady!'

Nessie patted his shoulder. 'Sin and wickedness bring their own hurt, laddie,' she said. 'You go for a walk, and when you come back we might have something to show you.'

'I can go alone?' Gareth was astonished and pleased.

'Yes, yes. Away with you.'

Gawain and the others were shooting at marks in the courtyard. Gareth walked over to them, anxious to share his treat. 'Nessie says I may go walking by *myself*, for the first time ever. Would you like to come too?'

Gawain and Agravaine laughed, with Gaheris joining in a few seconds later. Gareth was not aware of having said anything funny, so he stared in puzzlement.

Gawain grinned at him. 'Thanks for the thought, laddie, but if we came with you, how could you walk *alone*?'

'I wouldn't mind,' said Gareth eagerly, but the others had already turned back to their archery practice.

Since Nessie was not there to hold him back, Gareth went down to the shore. He clambered up on a flat rock, clasped his knees in his arms and sat looking out to sea. After a bit he began to shiver. The jewelled sparkle of the water dimmed and faded as if stained with milk, and the clouds clotted across the sun. A bitter wind rose, blowing from the south.

Gareth was about to leave his perch when he saw the seals. A group of six was swimming into shore, and as he watched, one veered from its companions. The mist thickened on the water, but in the brief glimpses Gareth had of the lone seal, it seemed to be making for his rock. Breathlessly, he waited. Time stretched, and the cold intensified. Gareth trembled and waited. And his patience was rewarded.

A sleek head with a whiskery muzzle appeared at

the edge of his rock and two intelligent dark eyes surveyed him. There was silence, as Gareth and the seal took one another's measure.

'Come up, little seal,' said Gareth softly. 'You must be cold in the water.'

The seal heaved itself onto the rock and shook the water from its thick pelt. 'You are a kind lad, Gareth of Orkney,' it said.

Gareth stared. The seal was gone, and on the rock beside him sat a stranger. The man was wearing a brown robe, and his hair and beard flowed down his front and back. He looked quite young, until Gareth met his gaze.

'My lord?' he stammered, for it seemed to him this must be the Apostle Peter at least. He would have thought it the Christ, but he knew the Christ had more to do than talk to an Orkney laddie, prince or not.

The man smiled. 'I am no lord, Gareth.'

'You are a selkie, sir?'

'I can be anyone you please.' The man waved his hand in a circular motion, and Gareth blinked up at his brother, Gawain. 'So, young sprig,' said Gawain easily. 'You got away from your nursemaid and came for a walk alone?'

Gareth rose shakily to his feet. 'Gawain? Is it you?'

'I am not your brother, sprig, but a seeming.' Gawain's image waved its hand, and there stood Nessie, her cap on crooked, her skirts kilted up. 'There, my lamb, have you enjoyed your walk? Come to old Nessie then, and give her a hug!'

Gareth sprang away. He staggered on the slippery surface of the rock and Nessie gripped his arm to steady him. She waved her hand, and became the stranger again.

'Who are you?' stammered Gareth.

The man smiled, ageless, merry and solemn together, and drew Gareth down to sit beside him. 'I am many things to many folk, Prince of Orkney. I am the old way, the gateway, the way of dreams and maybes.'

Gareth frowned, not understanding. 'What is your name, sir? Could it be Peter?'

'Some folk call me Ambrosius, but you may say "Merlin".'

'Merlin,' said Gareth. 'What are you, Merlin?'

'I am one who knows some things and hopes to learn others.'

'Do you know why it is so cold?'

'Cold things are afoot, Gareth. Old hatreds, old enmities, old wrongs have come together and set new wrongs in motion. Blood and blood that should never meet have mingled in the call of Camelot.'

Gareth wrinkled his brow, for the words meant very little and seemed to have nothing to do with him.

'Nor should you understand, at such a tender age.' Merlin smiled. 'There is time enough; the sprig of evil will take some time to become a tree. Soon the sun will come back and smile on the isles, and even on many-tower'd Camelot. Shall we wait for the sun together?'

'Tell me about Camelot,' said Gareth, but Merlin shook his head.

'Not today, young Gareth. But some day maybe, if you are fated to know. See, here is the sun. You must go home to your nurse.'

'What is that sound?' asked Gareth, as a low, mournful wailing came out of the south. 'Is it a horn, Merlin?'

'Nothing to trouble you, yet.'

'Shall I see you again?'

'Once and again.' Merlin rose and stretched, and his brown robes swirled themselves into feathers. A small brown hawk sprang from the rock, circled once then flew away to the south.

Gareth went home in a daze, to find Nessie still distracted and the place in an uproar. It was two hours more before he was taken to meet his new brother.

'What do you think of this ween?' asked Nessie.

'He is very fair,' said Gareth politely, looking at the scrawny baby. 'What is his name?'

Morgawse raised her head from the pillow. 'His name is Mordred,' she said. 'And he shall be my boy.'

94

For a while after Mordred's birth, Morgawse seemed more at peace. Nessie had less time to spend with Gareth, but she still went walking with him when she could spare an hour from tending the baby. At first, Gareth used to watch every seal and every distant bird, hoping to find Merlin, but as the months wore on, he remembered that strange encounter as a dream.

He wished he could dream it again, for in real life there was trouble. As Mordred grew from babyhood to become a small, demanding boy, Morgawse began to find fault with Nessie.

'You are never here when I need you!' she snapped, when Nessie came in with Gareth. 'Mordred has been crying this hour or more!' But on another day, she was saying, 'Can you never let me alone with my boy? Must you forever be hovering like some old cow who'd steal another's calf?'

Nessie stood it until Gareth was ten years old, and then she left Queen Morgawse's service. Gareth was bereft, but more unhappiness was coming. Gawain had angry words with Morgawse, and stormed away. And Gaheris and Agravaine soon followed his example. 'Take me with you!' pleaded Gareth to each in turn.

'I canna, my lamb,' said Nessie, and, 'Later, perhaps,' said Gawain, and Gaheris said, 'Some day.' Agravaine said nothing at all. After a wild quarrel with Morgawse, he was far too angry to speak.

Gareth was left alone. Mordred was too young to make a companion, and besides, he was usually with Morgawse. Gareth spent more and more time on the shore, staring south.

One day he stepped back on the flat rock where he had met Merlin on the day of Mordred's birth. He had stood there many times, so he had no hope that anything would happen. But then the gentle sea began to whip into wave peaks, racing before a barefoot southern breeze. The clouds were clotted across the sun, and the mist rose out of the water.

Gareth shivered with eagerness. He strained his eyes to peer through the mist, and he strained his ears for the sound of a distant horn. And out of the mist came the shadow of a boat, a small, flat barge with a mist-white rectangular sail. It drifted swiftly, silently, and in the stern sat a brown-robed figure with eyes both merry and sad.

'Hail, Prince of Orkney,' said Merlin. He anchored his craft and stepped up onto the rock.

'Merlin! I thought I had dreamed you.'

'Many have dreamed me, Gareth, and the dream goes on at Camelot.'

'Many-tower'd Camelot,' said Gareth, remembering. 'Is it far from here, Merlin?'

Merlin sighed, and folded himself to sit on the rock. 'It is far in the one sense, Gareth, but in another it is the very centre of things. Have you ever seen a spider's web? The strands are like the ways that lead to Camelot.'

'You talk in riddles,' said Gareth, laughing. 'What is it like at Camelot?'

'A shining court, bright with good intention,' said Merlin. 'Arthur Pendragon has built a dream that will last but a moment and forever.'

'Riddles again! Can't you say things plainly?'

'How can one speak of Camelot and make it plain? But I take your point, young Gareth. Much of the dream and all the sadness is still to come. For now there is laughter and jousting, and music in the halls.'

Gareth sighed with longing, and clasped his long, pale hands. 'Music, Merlin! I wish I could play a horn. And rescue a damosel, and be a gentle knight.'

Merlin was silent.

'And Arthur, my mother's brother, is king?' prompted Gareth.

'Her half-brother, for they shared the same mother, Lady Igraine. He is married to Guinevere, and all is merry.'

'My lady mother is never merry,' said Gareth.

Merlin sighed, as if all the weight of the world were on his shoulders. 'You have not much to be merry about yourself,' he said, 'and all because of choices made for you by others.'

'Why are you sad, Merlin? None of this is your fault.'

'Perhaps it is,' murmured Merlin. 'Men do what is

laid upon them, and wizards too. Tell me, young Gareth, if you were to see a drowning man out yonder, what would you do?'

'Try to help, of course,' said Gareth. 'Perhaps I would call for the fishermen, or cast a net for him to hold.'

'Would you stop to ask yourself if he were a good man, and worthy of saving?'

'No,' said Gareth.

'And should he turn out to be an ill kind of man to save, would you be sorry?'

'No, Merlin,' said Gareth. 'Men do what is laid upon them, as you might say. And so does a Prince of Orkney.'

Merlin slapped his knees with a shout of laughter. 'Well said, oh prince! Would you like to see your brothers?' He waved his arm in the familiar circle, and in the cloudy air appeared a disc of light. 'Look through, just as if it were a window,' said Merlin.

Eagerly, Gareth leaned forward. At first the scene was clouded, but a many-towered castle swam into view.

'Camelot,' said Merlin, and from the brilliant castle came the distant sound of a horn.

The castle sped closer, or perhaps it was Gareth travelling at such speed. In through the door he seemed to glide and there in a banqueting hall sat a king and his pensive queen.

'Arthur Pendragon and the Lady Guinevere,' said Merlin in his ear.

Along the tables sat knights and ladies, dressed in richer clothes than Gareth had ever imagined. At first he was dazzled by silk and brocade, but then he began to notice the faces. 'Gawain!' he whispered. 'Oh Merlin, there is my brother Gawain! How fine he looks! And there, beyond, are Gaheris and Agravaine. But how did they come to be there?'

'They have heard the call of Camelot,' said Merlin. 'It calls their blood, for good or ill, and the call has not ended yet.'

'Listen!' said Gareth, 'what is he saying?' Arthur the king had risen from his seat. The words came faintly to Gareth's ears, bright with promise.

'You are welcome, my friends, to our court and our table. I know too well of some dispute about whom shall sit at the head and the foot. Therefore I shall have a table made that has neither head nor foot. Then none may be said to be seated above the other.'

'Then all shall be as one!' cried Gawain. But another knight smote the table with his fist.

'The kitchen lads shall not be one with us, I hope!'

There was general laughter, but Arthur held up his hand. 'Sir Kay, a kindness to inferiors marks the truly gentle knight.'

The king's voice faded, as the vision died, and Gareth's last sight of that bright scene was of many knights, including his three brothers, on their feet, pounding with sword hilts and fists upon the table.

A herald winded a horn, and the sound cut bravely across the miles then faded into the mist. Gareth sighed with longing.

'What do you think of many-tower'd Camelot?' asked Merlin.

'It seems so merry and good!'

'And so it is, for now. And so it was meant to be.' Merlin's voice was sombre. 'And now I must go back.'

As before, the returning sun burned off the mist. Merlin rose in a swirl of robes, stepped back into his boat and was carried south.

Gareth stood on the rock and watched. 'Merlin!' he cried. 'Will I ever see you again?'

'Once and again, Prince of Orkney,' came Merlin's voice. 'We shall meet again, but it will not be in these isles.'

Gareth walked back towards his home. He knew he must leave it, and soon, for he, like others of his blood, had heard the call of Camelot. And men will do what it is laid upon them to do. Even a Prince of Orkney.

Author's Note

Gareth is one of the most attractive figures in the Arthurian stories. He was kind and brave, but he had a sense of humour. Some of the saintlier characters in legend suffer terribly when they fall off their pedestals, but Gareth never fell off. Maybe because he never knew he was standing on a pedestal.

I chose to write about Gareth thinking I would have more freedom with a lesser-known character. That was before I realised just how many better-known characters he was related to! I knew the tale of how Gareth arrived at Camelot in disguise, and worked as a kitchen lad. And how, guided by the Lady Linet, he rescued and married Linet's sister, the Lady Lyonesse. I also knew the tale of his death at the hands of Sir Lancelot during Guinevere's rescue. And, of course, I knew I wouldn't be using any of these, since they happened when Gareth was grown up.

I knew what kind of man he would become, but I still needed to know a little of his background to see what he might have been like as a boy. When I began my research, I found it difficult to pinpoint when Gareth's father died, or exactly where half-brother Mordred fitted into the family. In the end, I took the version of the legend that says King Lot died while Gareth was still a small child and that Queen Morgawse was not a very kindly mother. But how did Merlin come into the story? He wasn't there when I planned it, but in a way the whole situation with Arthur, Morgawse and Mordred was Merlin's fault. *He* had arranged for Morgawse's mother to give birth to Arthur, and Morgawse got revenge on Arthur by producing a son who would later kill his father. And then there was blameless Gareth, a nice little boy caught up in all this heavy revenge scenario. Would Merlin feel responsible for Gareth's situation? Did he visit out of genuine sympathy, or was he just stirring the pot? After all, Gareth had to get to Camelot *somehow*, so he could work in the kitchen and rescue the Lady Lyonesse. Perhaps Merlin's motives don't matter for, as Gareth says in my story, 'A man will do what is laid on him to do. Even a Prince of Orkney.'

GUINEVERE, OR THE SLEEPING BEAUTY

Isobelle Carmody

'I swear that bird is watching you, Vera,' Alyson said.

Vera barely heard her, so intent was she on the tiny book resting upon the layers of brown paper and bubble wrap that it had come cocooned in. She was almost afraid to open it for fear that the thick, brittle pages would crumble under her breath, and yet if she did not, she would never know what it was. The legend had long ago worn off the dark cloth-bound cover, leaving a few shreds of gold that she suspected might be gold leaf. No wonder the book had been sent to her by special courier rather than being trusted to the ordinary post like other parcels from her guardian.

'I'm serious, Vera,' Alyson's voice broke into her thoughts. 'It's been sitting on the sill for five minutes and it hasn't taken its beady little eyes off you.'

'It's probably admiring its reflection,' Vera murmured, deciding that her guardian would have warned her if the book should not be opened. He had always been meticulous and even slightly pedantic with the penned and occasionally eccentric instructions that had accompanied some of the other gifts. She had no idea of his age, but she had formed the impression of a scholarly man with little experience of children or young women.

She took up the silver dagger letter opener he had sent her for Christmas the year before and slid it carefully between the heavy cover and the pages inside. One of her teachers had said the dagger was a real weapon whose edge had been deliberately blunted, but she did not think this very likely.

'Vera!' Alyson shouted, making her jump slightly. 'Maybe it's some sort of omen and it can't flap away until you look at it. Aren't crows birds of ill omen?'

'Messengers,' Vera said absently.

Alyson stepped around the front of the desk and said determinedly and slowly, 'Look at the window.' She pointed.

Vera turned, opening her mouth to make some ironic comment about needing directions to the window, but the words died on her lips, for there was a large crow huddled right up against the glass with its black wicked-looking beak turned sideways and it really did look at if it was staring in at her. Then, somewhere, a door slammed shut and the bird flapped lazily away.

Vera shook her head and turned back to the book. 'Will you go and bird watch somewhere else, Aly? I'm trying to concentrate.'

'You're so conscientious,' Alyson complained, crossing to the mirror and considering her strawberry blonde gamine-cut hair and pert pretty face with vague dissatisfaction.

'I'm not conscientious. I'm interested,' Vera said, easing the book cover open. She winced at the sound of a sharp crack from the spine and hoped the binding was sewn as well as glued. Judging by the sticky powder lying on the paper, the glue had gone through the dust-to-dust part of its incarnation. 'Besides, how can anyone be conscientious about a present?'

'That's just what I mean!' Alyson said. 'You treat a birthday present as if it were homework, and what sort of present is that to give a sixteen-year-old girl anyway? A horrible, musty old book! If I were you I'd start worrying about those accountants that look after your money. I bet they've embezzled the fabulous fortune your parents left you and they sent that to keep you quiet while they take off to the Bahamas or Bermuda or wherever it is that embezzlers go.'

'It's an antique,' Vera said.

'So is your guardian to have sent that to you. Now a decent guardian would have sent you tickets to a Scan concert. Or a full-length black leather jacket.'

'I hate Scan and I don't care about clothes or how I look.'

'That's exactly what I mean,' Alyson said in an aggrieved voice. 'I mean you can say you don't care how you look *because* of how you look! Wear a paper bag and people will still be struck dumb by how beautiful you are. Did you see that new science teacher this morning? I swear his Adam's apple was doing the rumba when he spoke to you. I mean, look at you! Creamy skin that has never seen a pimple in its life, masses of silky, rose-gold curls that never had a bad hair day and a mouth that might as well be an advertisement for kissing. You even have green eyes! How unfair is that! You know how rare green eyes are?'

'If rare is beautiful then this book is exquisite …' Vera said firmly, disappointed to find that there was nothing on the front page, although it looked as if there had once been a handwritten inscription on the inside page.

'A book is not beautiful. It is trashy and exciting or it is deeply profound and therefore barely comprehensible to ordinary mortals. People are beautiful or not. Mostly not,' Alyson added with a faint wistfulness that betrayed the truth of her, hidden behind the brazen manner and clever wit.

'I need a magnifying glass,' Vera muttered.

Alyson was tired of striking dramatic poses with no audience. She flopped onto the tapestried chair in the corner of the room, her smile fading as she studied her friend, thinking of the coma in which she had lain for months, after the death of her parents. Vera had only mentioned it the once, saying that she had wakened as if newborn and had to be taught to speak and understand the world all over again. Sometimes Vera imagined her as she must have been; a sleeping beauty that doctors and nurses would come to gaze at in wonder and in secret. Then she had awakened, revealing that she was beautiful inside as well as out. That was how it was possible to bear her physical beauty. Vera was not proud or boastful for all her wealth, and she was wonderfully generous with her money and her possessions other than the things her guardian had sent. And she was kind. She would listen to a person moan on for hours, just as if their woes were actually interesting to her. Or maybe she was interested.

'So what is the book anyway?' Alyson asked at last, affectionately.

Catching the tone, Vera sent her a smile of such sweetness that Alyson caught her breath. 'I don't know,' she admitted disconsolately. 'I've gone over two pages and there's no title page. It doesn't look as if any of the pages have fallen out, but I daren't push the book open any harder to make sure because the glue is already cracking.'

'Surely it's sewn?' Alyson levered herself up and came over, and a faint smell rose to her nostrils as she leaned over the little book. It was not musty after all. That had been poetic licence. In fact, the smell was rather like that of pressed flowers that had once been beautifully scented.

Vera turned another page and both girls drew in a breath to find it all written over. 'Why it's not a printed book at all …'

'What horrible handwriting,' Alyson cried. 'It's as bad as yours. Hey! You know, I've just figured out what this is!' The words held such conviction that Vera looked up at her. 'It's your guardian taking his revenge. He's telling you why he never wrote back.'

Vera looked down so that her friend would not see the little stab of unhappiness she felt at the reminder that her guardian had never answered one of her carefully penned requests for an interview, or at least for some information about her parents. There had been no reply, but she had gone on sending them, until finally a polite note had come from the head of the accounting firm handling her trust, asking that she not send any more letters to her guardian. She had been too humiliated and disheartened to persist. She hadn't told this to Alyson for fear of being cast as the main character in a contorted and Dickensian tale of an orphaned child.

'The ink has faded badly,' she merely said now. 'I wonder if the library would know how to make it easier to read.'

'I'd try the science department,' Alyson suggested mischievously.

Which was how, half an hour later, Vera found herself ushered into the small sitting room of the Head of Sciences, Mr Nicholas Farrenby. She was very apologetic when she realised that he was having tea with his nephew who was visiting from Cambridge. She offered to return later, but he insisted that she sit and explain the reason for her visit. Alyson had declined to come and so Vera was able to succinctly explain her problem.

'Well,' Mr Farrenby said thoughtfully, 'there are certain chemicals which might be used to bring up the ink, either by direct application or by exposure to the fumes, but if the book is as old as you say, I doubt that your guardian would approve.' His smile reminded them both of how much the school benefited from the largesse of her guardian, which was, of course, why his occasional requests were honoured without demur. 'Therefore, it seems to me that you might be wisest to begin by trying some less potentially damaging means. Coloured lights perhaps, or tinted filters. You may be able to borrow the latter from the photography laboratory.'

Vera rose and took her leave gravely, and only after

the door closed, did Mr Farrenby turn to his nephew who was shaking his head as if to clear it after someone had given him a hard knock. 'Was I dreaming or did a vision of beauty just visit us?' Maxwell Farrenby asked.

'I am afraid so,' Mr Farrenby said. 'I'm sorry you were here, lad.'

'Are you mad? I mean, I'm sorry Uncle, but what can you mean?'

'I mean what I said, as I always do. I wish you hadn't seen her. I am afraid it will trouble you.'

'Trouble me?'

'It has done so inevitably when any young man sees her. That is why her guardian sent her here, of course. She is dangerous and endangered, and this boarding school is remote and strict and there are no male students and no young male teachers. Though it is bad enough with some of the not so young men.' He was thinking of the new science master.

'But … I can't believe you're serious. You are, aren't you?' Max liked his uncle and was struck by the fact that the older man looked not only worried but also sad. 'Whatever is the matter? Is there something wrong with her?'

'Nothing other than that she is so dreadfully beautiful that her life will be marred by it. No-one will ever manage to treat her normally. Can you possibly imagine the efforts we have gone through here to shield her from the effects of her freakish beauty? That was the express wish of her guardian, and he has paid us handsomely for it, not only by funding the modernisation of the plumbing and heating systems in the dormitories, and roof repairs to the chapel, but also by enabling several programs of research of which a school would not normally be capable, thereby drawing together teachers of the calibre that make this a truly striking place to work and live. Nevertheless, I cannot help but pity the girl. Most of us here do.'

'Incredible,' the young man said, not quite sure to what he was referring, but at the same time, the image of the young woman shone in his mind like a flame and he began wondering if it would be possible for him to visit his uncle again the following weekend, or perhaps even midweek if he cut one of his classes. He could contrive to take a stroll across the grounds during lunchbreak. He had not been formally introduced to the girl, a fact which had initially puzzled him, but he felt confident that he could get away with introducing himself and passing the time of day. He found himself longing to hear her voice again and to have her name upon his lips.

'I fear that it will not be possible for you to come here again, my boy, and for that I am truly sorry,' his uncle said sorrowfully.

'Green!' Alyson cried in delight. 'Who would have thought it.'

Vera strove to flatten the crumpled cellophane and said, 'Let me see. There's a smudged bit and then it says *Martin has suggested I keep this ... diary. He says it will help me learn to think better and maybe my daughter ...*'

'Oh my god, it's from your mother!' Alyson screamed.

Vera burst out laughing. 'You idiot, how could it be? This is hundreds of years old.'

Alyson looked taken aback, then she shrugged and laughed. 'All right, read on then.'

Vera did. '*Maybe my daughter will ... read it ...* then something something something.'

'Oh that's deep.'

'Shh. *I have never seen such binding nor such fine paper in my life. I think it might be ... en ...* engraved maybe. *I asked him if he had obtained it from ... from* somewhere, and then there's a smudged word. It must be a place.'

'Go on with it.'

'*It is very like him to be so cryptic . I do ... loath him? No, love* him, maybe. The whole bottom bit of this page is unreadable.' She turned the page carefully. '*Ysabeau says that he knows everything but Martin says it is not true. Yet sometimes when he looks at me, I swear she did have it right. Once he saw me with Abillard who is very ... handsome, and he called me aside and said that a true matching of souls such as he sees for me happens once in a thousand years, and that to even dream of less is to lessen what will come. I do not know ... half of what he means, and yet when* he speaks in such a grave and meaningful way to me, I sometimes wonder if he has seen some fell future for me. Though I do not know how a future in which I will meet my mated soul can be bad … something something something.'

'Oh, don't start that again, and just when it was getting interesting,' Alyson said.

'Shh. Let me try the next page. No, that's faded like the first one.' She turned another page using the tip of the ornamental dagger and to her astonishment, she found herself looking at a beautiful little sketch of the very dagger in her hand!

'This is … this is creepy,' Alyson said.

'Probably the letter opener is a copy of the original that this was drawn from,' Vera said, but she felt herself that it was the same dagger. Perhaps her guardian had obtained the dagger in the drawing, then had later managed to get this diary which referred to it. There were obscure links sometimes to be found between the gifts sent over the two years since she had wakened. Sometimes she had felt there might be some secret message to be found in these links, if only she had been clever enough to decipher it.

There was writing underneath the picture and she shifted the cellophane and read, 'Martin brought me a gift today, which is so lovely that I have given myself leave to sketch it. He says that the … hilt is designed to match the very same blade that … I can't read a couple of words, then won from the earth? No that doesn't make sense.'

'I don't think it's Martin,' Alyson interrupted. 'I think that's an "e".'

'Mertin? I don't think that can be right. Oh well. *Mertin says it is a betrothal gift from my soul mate, whom I am to meet in a week. A knight will be sent to conduct me and my ladies to his palace* ... Oh, how lovely! She is to be a queen! I wonder which one.'

'Mertin must be her father or brother. Or maybe he's her guardian.'

There was a tightness behind Vera's eyes as she turned the next page, and she wondered if she was getting a headache. The page was smudged and so was the next and twenty more, then, as she was coming to the last few pages, suddenly the words were clear again. 'Mertin or Martin, *says that the world of faerie diminishes and when it goes, enchantment will perish and humankind fall inevitably into darkness and despair. He says that my destiny is to bring together the world of faerie and the world of men, so that one may not die and the other not fall. I do not know what he means.*'

'That makes two of us,' Alyson muttered.

Vera turned another page and shook her head to find it smeared and illegible. She went on turning pages until she came to one that was only part filled, yet this was readable. The pages after it were blank and so this, it seemed, was the final page of the journal. '*Last night I dreamed that I was killed. Ysabeau said dreams can be omens and that I should take care not to turn my back on my husband. I snapped at her, for the dream made me afraid, but I can not fear him who is the* mate of my soul and who will in three days make me from child to woman. There's another bit I can't read, then I have decided that I will write no more in this book, for will I not henceforth confide my intimate thoughts to my love? Mertin had agreed to dispose of this book for I have writ things within in it that may cause sorrow or harm to others if it were happened upon. How strangely he started when I said that otherwise, if he chose, he might keep it safe for the future.' Vera looked up. 'That's all.'

'What a pity we couldn't read any of the part where she met her true love,' Alyson lamented.

Vera's headache had arrived. It felt as if her temples were swollen out with the force of it, hammering at her brain. She felt as if her head might explode. 'I must read it properly. I'm going to see if I can get a town pass tomorrow. I will go into the antiquarian bookshop and see if they can tell me if it can be restored.'

'A town pass? They'll never give it to you. Potts is so stingy with passes. You practically have to be dying before they let you even go to the hospital.'

Vera frowned, knowing this to be true. The school was very strict about visits to the nearest town, which was in fact little more than a village. 'Nevertheless,' she said.

Alyson's eyes widened at this rare sign of rebelliousness in a girl whom teachers described as biddable. 'We'll have to sneak off. I'm game if you are.'

'You needn't come, Alyson. If I'm caught there will be a real row.'

'And let my best friend risk life and reputation all alone? We'd be better to go right after breakfast because they won't worry about us until midafternoon rollcall. We might even manage to be back by then.'

'What about lunch roll?'

'I'll ask Liane to cover for us. She's doing the roll this week.'

Carefully, Vera closed the book and began to rewrap it. Her heart beat strangely fast and, on impulse, she put the dagger in her pocket. Maybe the bookseller would know something about the markings on the top part of the blade.

By midmorning, they had walked the five kilometres to town and, as it was a warm day, they were both hot and had removed their jackets. They had elected not to wear their school uniforms so as not to attract attention, but as they entered the outskirts of the town, Alyson could feel them being stared at. It was not her eccentrically tie-dyed clothes that was drawing attention, nor the fact that the girls were strangers. It was Vera's beauty which, away from the dull grey surrounds of the school, seemed to blaze out like a torch. But glancing at the lovely profile, it struck Alyson that her friend looked slightly ill. 'Are you all right?' she asked.

'I've just got a bit of a headache. I slept badly last night.'

'You were probably nervous about today.'

Vera shook her head, sending the myriad of silky curls swaying and tumbling, glinting in the sunlight. A boy riding past them almost fell off his bicycle in his effort to turn back and look at her. She said, 'I dreamed of two knights riding at one another in a forest, and then they were on the ground fighting with swords. It was misty and I could hear the sound of them grunting and the clang of their swords. One man was killed at last and the other rode off. Then I was in a castle and I could hear a man weeping. It was the man who killed the one in the forest. He was leaning over a girl lying dead on the ground. There was another man lying dead a little way off. Then all of a sudden the dead man turned his head and I saw that he was quite young. He began laughing; a horrible cruel laughter, but you could tell that he was in pain as well. Then there was a voice saying that it was time for me to wake, and I did.'

'It's that book,' Alyson said. 'The girl who wrote it was talking about dreams too, remember?'

Vera said nothing, because she did not want to explain that for the last two years, indeed ever since she had wakened from her coma, she had been having snatches of this same dream. It was only the last few weeks that the dreams had filled out and connected. If she did not feel so strangely tired today, she might have worried about it. But as it was, she found it hard to do more than put one foot in front of another. The heat was making her feel feverish and she was just beginning to wonder if she was not really becoming ill, when Alyson spotted the bookseller. The inside of the basement shop was beautifully cool and the older woman behind the counter, despite her severe appearance, was kind and helpful. She took the book from them, unwrapped it reverently and asked if they could come back after lunch. She might have something to tell them then.

'We might as well go and have a drink,' Alyson announced when they were outside. 'I'm boiling to death out ... Hey! Look, it's your pet omen.'

Vera looked up, squinting against the blaze of light, but she was too slow. All she could make out in the blinding glare was a flash of inky feathers splayed like claws and then the bird was gone from sight. Too hot to speak, she followed Alyson into The Sugar Shop and stood as her friend ordered them both strawberry shakes. Alyson led the way to the furthermost shady corner of the shop carrying both shakes. She had been a little unnerved at how many people not only stared at Vera, but followed after them. So far, not more than a few steps, then they would shake their heads and seem to come to themselves and turn away. Preoccupied by her thoughts, she was almost at the table when she noticed there was an old man sitting in the pool of shadows at the far end. 'Sorry,' she said and began to back away, but a gnarled hand made a scooping movement and a ring flashed in a strand of sunlight. A white opal or an enormous pearl.

'Please join me,' the man invited in a rich, compelling voice.

Alyson would have refused but Vera slipped by her and sat down leaving her no alternative. She set the shakes down but could not bring herself to sit.

'Be at peace, child. Sit and you shall have a story that you will never forget.' These words were so strange and unlikely that Alyson found herself obeying. She sat opposite her friend who was staring down the table at the old man with the sort of expression people got on their faces when they were trying to remember something that they had forgotten, and yet knew very well.

A notion, absurd and yet compelling, struck Alyson. 'You're Vera's guardian.'

'Bravo,' the old man said, clapping his hands like a child, and yet there was nothing childish about the face whose features were becoming clearer as their eyes adjusted to the light. Or was it that the shadows were actually dispersing like mist? He turned to Vera. 'Indeed, I have been waiting for my ward.'

'Waiting?' Vera echoed. 'But I … did not get any message. It was only by chance that we came in here.'

'You came because I sent the book so that it would arrive yesterday, the day before your birthday.'

'No, her birthday is not until —' Alyson began.

'Today is your sixteenth birthday and it is time for you to awaken and to fulfil your destiny at last.'

'I tried to read the book,' Vera murmured, seeming not to notice the oddness of the old man's declaration. 'Most of the words were smudged or too faded to read …'

'I am afraid that is my doing,' the old man said. 'I could not leave your words to be read by those who might come to guess who had written it. But the book did its work, if you are here.'

'My words!' Vera whispered. 'But how is that possible? I'd have to be hundreds of years old!'

'One thousand and sixteen years old, to be precise.'

'That's impossible,' Alyson said flatly. There was a flash of whiteness than she hoped was a smile and not a baring of teeth.

'The gifting of the book was but a whim of mine when I gave it,' the old man said. 'Or so I thought it. When you gave it back to me, I kept it out of sentiment. Later I was glad of it, for it was potent with you. It could have taken the entire waking spell, but it was safer to infuse a number of objects with parts of the spell, and link them so that only when together, would they restore your memory. The book was the last of it. You have the dagger with you?'

'Then it is a dagger?'

'Your betrothed sent it you as a token. I cast a

protection spell upon it and it operates even now, so you should keep it with you always.'

'Her *betrothed* sent it?' That was Alyson.

'Arthur,' the old man said. 'King Arthur.'

'You mean Arthur who pulled the sword out of the stone and built a round table …' Alyson's mockery faltered when she saw the expression of shock on Vera's face, the sour cream pallor of her cheeks.

The old man said mildly, 'The same Arthur whom tales say was betrayed by his beloved wife, Guinevere, with Lancelot of the Lake; Arthur who fought that same Lancelot and was slain by him. Arthur whose wife and queen was then supposed to have left Camelot with Mordred.'

'Ah, sweet heaven,' Vera gasped. 'That was the dream! Lancelot killed Arthur in a sword fight, and then he killed Mordred and … there was a girl in the dream who he had killed. Guinevere. But last night, when I dreamed, for the first time I saw her face and it was … me!'

'No, my dear,' the old man said softly, taking Vera's long slender fingers in his own. He patted her hands as if they were frightened little animals, then laid them in her lap. 'It was not you, Guinevere, though Lancelot and poor mad Mordred believed it. Mordred, who had long been twisted and tormented by the very powers that Arthur sensed were his truest enemy.'

'He said that he felt that there was a secret corrupting

force which opposed all that was good in men and women and made them do evil,' Vera whispered. 'He said it was a force that could not be countered with steel, but only with dreams and beauty such as would be represented by Camelot and all that it symbolised.'

'That force he sensed existed and exists. Indeed, it feels itself to have won.'

'I don't understand,' Vera whispered. There were tears on her cheeks now and a wounded look in her eyes. 'The stories say that I betrayed him but I have no memory of it, though I remember Lancelot. Who could forget him? He came to bring me to my lord and he was handsome and lithe and strong. Half of my ladies were swooning over him. Arthur said that he knew how to dance with death and I think it was true. But I did not love him.'

'No,' the old man said. 'You did not, nor did you betray your love, though the world has had to be allowed to believe it. And yet there were magics in the legends I wove about you and Arthur and Lancelot. The embryo of beauty that was Camelot was not entirely extinguished because of those stories, and of course the truth was hidden in the inconsistencies.'

'Do you mean …' Alyson began, then she stopped because she did not know what she meant to say. The old man looked at her with grave courtesy until she plucked up the courage to ask, 'Are you saying that she … that Vera, is … was … Guinevere?'

The old man turned to Vera, who said, 'Oh, I remember being she of the bright hair and the ringing laugh, whom Arthur loved when first he saw her. I was but thirteen when I was given to him to wive. He had not expected love and nor had I. We were the dutiful children of kings, yet I remember the burning of our souls when we kissed. I did not betray my lord.'

'No,' the old man said. 'It would have been impossible for two souls mated as yours and Arthur's were, to have wrought such a thing. You remember no more because three days before your fourteenth birthday, you received a gift —'

Vera gasped. 'The spindle. I remember. A lovely thing. I had never used one, but Arthur sent it me.'

'He did not. It was a poisonous gift, born of long-steeped hatred and jealousy. Of course you pricked your finger. I came upon you lying there. Any other would have thought you dead, but I alone knew that you were not human, but faerie. It was this that held the poison at bay, yet I could not purge it, and so I sent you into a sleep so deep that it was as if you were dead, knowing you must lie thus until whensoever the dark poison in your veins lost its potency. How I cursed and wept for a foolish old man's passion, which had seen me absent when I was most needed to keep you safe. To keep safe the dream that was a rare and precious child of faerie capable of mating with a human so long as that human was her soul mate. As Arthur was. The Lords of Faerie had long wrought to bring you into existence, just as I schemed to bring Arthur to the world. You were to be the grail the fairy folk offered to the world, so that the beauty which was faerie should not die, but would mingle and enrich human blood, and now you slept.'

'There is a fairytale about a sleeping princess and a spindle …' Alyson murmured.

The old man nodded. 'I wove legends about the spindle and the sleeping beauty, but somehow they split away from the tale of Guinevere and the great betrayal, and became a story in their own right. Stories are a little like magic, I find. The best of them are not entirely tame and so you can never be quite sure what they will make and what will be made of them. And stories contain their own sleeping beauty. Their own enchantment.'

'What happened next?' Alyson prompted.

The old man's eyes had a blind sheen as if they looked inward now. 'It seemed that all was lost yet I could not let you die. I sent your sleeping form outside of time so that you would not age, and I chose not to reveal what had been done to you, knowing that the moment the truth was known, they would bend all of their malevolent power to find and destroy you. I told myself that Arthur would have it so, and I let him and the world believe that she who had taken the place she had long and bitterly desired, was you.'

'Ysabeau!' Vera almost sighed.

'Ysabeau? That name was in the book,' Alyson said.

Vera looked at her. 'She was my sister. My half-sister. My father, King Leodogrance, sired her upon Dame Kellert who was a midwife about the palace. Ysabeau was born the same night as I, and we were both very like to our father. Ysabeau disliked Arthur, I remember. She said he was a dreaming fool. We fell out over it, and yet she insisted on remaining with me as a maid.'

'She sent the spindle to kill you, and then she took your place. None ever knew it and she never knew what became of the body, for I contrived a fire to hide my theft. Once she realised that Arthur could not love her, though he believed her to be you, she took pleasure in betraying him. He blamed himself, poor man. He could not understand how such love as he had felt could die. His inconstancy bewildered and grieved him. He did not blame her whom he thought to be you, for taking Lancelot as a lover. He only urged discretion for the sake of the dream of Camelot that was his only solace now. Lancelot had been in love with you since he first saw you, of course, for all men are drawn to enchantment as inexorably as a flower turns to the sunlight.'

'My poor Arthur,' Vera said.

'I think he came to doubt his dream of Camelot because the dream of love had proven false,' the old man said heavily. 'He tried to let Ysabeau escape, even after all was falling to ruin. He sent word for Lancelot to ride in at night and steal her away, but Lancelot did not receive the message. And so Lancelot came riding to battle. When Lancelot came to find the false Guinevere after he had slain the king, he found that she was with Mordred and he slew her before she could tell him that she had been taken against her will. Mordred taunted him with this even as he died of his wounds.'

'A lot of stories say that Lancelot didn't kill Guinevere. That she lived and went to live in a convent, or that she became the high priestess of a secret order,' Alyson murmured. She was startled to find that she had been drinking her milkshake.

The old man nodded. 'The truth has a way of leaking from the locked casket of a lie. Anyone reading or hearing the story of the great betrayal knew instinctively that it was flawed. The flaw lay in the fact that Guinevere betrayed Arthur whose heart was so pure that the faerie sword allowed him to draw it from the earth. Of course she would not betray him. She could not betray her mated soul.'

'But … umm … how did Ve … Guinevere come to be here?' Alyson asked.

The old man smiled at her. 'Do you fear to name me, child?'

'Merlin, not Mertin,' Vera murmured.

'Yes. I have many names but that is the most commonly used. In the oldest tongues it renders as teller of tales. As to your question, I brought Guinevere to this time because the poison had at last lost its power. I brought her first to what your world calls a hospice. When she woke from her coma the doctors used their abilities to restore her to health and mobility and, believing her to be amnesiac, they taught her the ways and language of this time far better than I could have done.'

'Why did you tell me all of this? I was robbed of my life and my love and if what you say is true about Arthur and I, the world was robbed of its dream. So why torment me with the knowledge of it? I was content enough without it.'

'You were sleeping,' Merlin said sternly. 'And do not imagine that your existence here has been an easy thing to devise. It was difficult to know what to do with you because in this time which is barren of enchantment, the beauty that is Guinevere would be even more potent. I had to work very hard to create an environment where you could exist and grow in relative peace. Your school is all but my own construction. A lovely gilded cage.'

Guinevere asked, 'Can't you take me back to him?'

'I cannot take you back in time, child. Arthur is dead and the age of Camelot is passed into legend and myth. You must live the remainder of your life in this time.'

'But what is the use of it?' Guinevere said softly. 'I am a freak here. I see that now. Better if I had died or slept forever.'

Merlin smiled. 'I am wise and I know much, but there are forces at work in the world that are beyond even me. I did not choose this time, and yet by chance or fate or destiny, I have learned that the soul which once was in Arthur, has been reborn into another man. I have not power enough left to seek him out for I will soon pass beyond the eye of time. But I offer you this hope, Guinevere. Find him who was once Arthur, and kiss awake the dream of beauty; your love will lift the eyes of the slouching beast that humanity has become.'

'You will die?' Alyson asked.

'That is a limited term and rather unbeautiful, but yes.' He looked back to Guinevere and allowed himself, just once, to feel the full lovely force of her enchanted beauty. It smote him like a blow and his heart faltered in his chest. 'He that was Arthur will not know you exist, of course, but you will recognise him by his pure heart and his dreams that will set the world to yearning again for Camelot.'

He rose and both girls stared up at him in disbelief. 'It is time,' he said regretfully and slightly breathlessly. Alyson noticed there was a bluish tinge to his lips. 'I would say that I am sorry to go, and that I would have wished to see beauty wake, yet it would not be true. I am weary and would fain let my story end.' He touched Guinevere's creamy velvet cheek with a long finger. Then he looked at Alyson and smiled. 'Shall I tell your future, child? If Guinevere finds her soul mate, you will witness the kiss and will be the first awakened to beauty by it.'

Then, just like that, they were alone, two girls sitting before two milkshakes, one almost drunk to the dregs. They sat silent until the waitress came over and asked them pointedly if they wanted anything more, then they paid and walked outside. It was dusk.

'There'll be hell to pay at school,' Guinevere sighed.

Alyson gave her a startled look. Then she laughed and tucked her arm through her friend's. 'The way I see it, Vera, is that we have a prince to find, and I don't mind telling you that I'm glad you are to go hunting him and don't have to wait in a tower to be rescued. I always hated that bit in stories.'

Neither of the girls noticed a crow land on a telephone wire overhead and watch them, its sharp beak turned to press against the glossy black of its wings.

AUTHOR'S NOTE

When I was asked if I would like to write a childhood story about one of the characters from the Camelot legend, I felt the obvious choice to be Morgana, or Merlin, two powerful and ambivalent characters. But in the end I chose Guinevere, because she seemed the least interesting of the characters.

Guinevere had always struck me not only as a pawn but also as a peculiar woman for two great men to love so deeply and desperately, given that she was faithless. I have read many books where, while I was reading, I was convinced that passion was reason enough for her behaviour, but in truth my own morality is harder and colder than that, and insists that love and honour should be inseparable. One could love another but not act upon it. So for me, the legend was always flawed. I thought that I would write about Guinevere to find out what really motivated and moved her.

I set out by trying to learn something about her childhood, but in fact there was little to learn and especially, since I was living in Prague at the time, almost no way to get information. So I emailed friends, who sent me tidbits. The first thing that interested me was from the French version of the story, which tells that Guinevere had an exact twin who took her place for a time. That was when I conceived the idea that the Guinevere loved so deeply by two men, was in fact two women. Then another friend sent a different version of the legend and I was surprised to read there that Lancelot killed Guinevere for going off with Mordred, and I decided to use this in my story as well.

When I sat down to write the story, I saw a room in a boarding school overlooking a remote wilderness, and two schoolgirls being watched by a black bird sitting on a windowsill. The story thus became a time-travel story and also a retelling of the Sleeping Beauty fairytale. I love it when stories do as this one did, and take me over. And I love having found that I can believe that Guinevere was a true heroine, with a strange and unexpected destiny, far from the tragic tangle of the past. I always did hate tragic endings, especially ones where everyone dies. But as you can tell, I am too much of a realist to write a happy ending without suggesting at least a shadow.

LANCELOT

Sophie Masson

The land under the Lake had been home to the child for as long as he could remember, yet he knew he did not come from there. Occasionally, in terrifying, puzzling nightmares, he caught glimpses of some other place, oddly familiar. Walls rearing high, so high they touched the sky, a sky of a strange greenish black; figures moving jerkily; then a vast roar, a thrashing as if of a giant tail, a voice calling, crying; then utter silence, and a great black mass advancing, sinuous and inescapable. But he did not speak of these nightmares to anyone, for he could scarcely even put words to them.

He was happy in the Lake, living under the Lady's protection in the gorgeous halls underwater. Water was his element. And there were so many places to explore, wonderful things to look at, and magic that appeared at the touch of a finger, the breath of a wish. He was a reserved, dreamy child, but with a core of wildness to him that showed in sudden flashes of fiery behaviour. He didn't just explore the Lake, he also spent a lot of time reading illustrated books about strange lands above the water. He did not lack for company, either; there was a pack of quiet but playful red-eared white dogs that followed him everywhere, and the Lady of the Lake, her sisters, and her servants were unfailingly kind and affectionate.

But his favourite time of all was when, on moonlit nights, they would swim up together, the Lady, her sisters and the child, up into the strange world above the water. Water stretched everywhere, for this was a place between two waters — the deep stillness of the Lake, the hiss and stir of mighty ocean. The sky met the waters imperceptibly, and the land between these waters was flat silvery sand, with reeds growing thickly by the edge of the Lake and rolling dunes towards the ocean. It was utterly uninhabited by human beings: not a house, not a hut, not even a fisherman's boat to be seen anywhere. No large animals lived there either, though there were many small bustling things, like water-rats, and thousands of birds. And insects; large armies of them rustled and bustled in the reeds; and legions of sea-creatures such as crabs scuttled about on the sands, while oysters and mussels clung to rocks on the beach and at the mouth of the Lake, and fish of all colours and shapes and sizes swam in both the fresh and salty waters.

He would wander among the reeds at the water's edge, beating at them with a stick, forging himself a path through them, telling himself stories as he went. He would get down on his belly to watch some of the busy insect rituals, which only halted if his shadow, a giant's shadow, fell over them. He imagined that their mounds and grass fortifications were like the castles he had seen in the books he read, and that the little insect-warriors and ladies were undergoing complicated ordeals and wondrous adventures. The birds that swooped down greedily to cause havoc among the insect settlements were ogres and black knights bent on destruction, or else gorgeous visitors from another world.

There was that about this empty place and its remote power that fired his imagination, quite unlike the Lake and its known and familiar magic. The land was unknowable, mysterious, calling to him beyond words, almost beyond feelings …

So absorbed was he that he never noticed the Lady and her sisters watching him, talking in low voices about him. He did not see that their calm eyes were sometimes filled with the expectation of the pain of loss, and of the path he must take when he was grown. His childhood was blessed; and it was filled with waiting. This also he did not know, but carried it within him, like a gift, and a curse.

Life had gone on for him thus for many years, until the day of his thirteenth birthday. That morning, he woke feeling different. He did not understand the way he felt, the harsh knocking of his heart against his ribs, the chills that crept over him from head to foot, the way his scalp crinkled with ice and fire, and his throat choked with some odd constriction.

When he came into the dining hall, he found that the Lady and all of her sisters were already there waiting for him. The Lady was at the head of the table, as always, but her face was still and more grave than usual, and there was an expression in her eyes that the boy did not recognise. He knelt before her to receive her blessing, but instead of touching him lightly on the shoulder, as usual, she put her hand gently on his hair and stroked his head, very briefly.

'My dear child,' said the Lady, in her deep, gentle voice, 'you must have been lonely all these years.'

'Lonely?' he said wonderingly, then choked with a sudden insight. Was that what the strange feeling had been — a realisation of just what he'd never felt, all these years: loneliness. Had things been ordered in the

Lake so that he would never know that until this morning? But why?

'We could not do otherwise, you see,' said the Lady sadly. 'Oh, Lancelot, there was nothing else we could do.'

They did not often call him by his name, preferring to term him by many small endearments, like Tadpole, and Little One, and Boy. But he liked to hear it when they did; a lilting name, soft and billowing like the Lake. Today, it sent another tremor through him; not a tremor of loneliness realised, but something else, something he knew at once, though he could not have said why. Excitement. Expectation. Something momentous truly about to happen.

'I understand,' he said, though of course he didn't.

'Lancelot, my very dear, do you remember anything before you came here?'

The glimpses of that past life, puzzling and frightening, streaked across Lancelot's mind like a falling star. He winced, and replied, 'A little. A very little.'

'Will you tell me what it is you remember?' she said.

So he told her, haltingly at first, then with greater and greater force, as the pictures gathered in his mind and burst the dam of his long silence. There was a quietness when he had finished, and then the Lady gently said, 'Why didn't you tell us you remembered all this, Lancelot?'

'You never asked me before,' he said simply.

She nodded. 'Very well.' She beckoned to a servant. 'Bring them here.'

At these words, Lancelot's heart hammered so hard against his ribs that he thought it would leap out of his chest. 'Who … who …' he stammered, while the excitement in him grew and grew, pushing out the fear of the memories.

'Your cousins, Lancelot. They are to live under the Lake with you for a year, and then —'

'My cousins!' said Lancelot, daring to interrupt her. Under his thatch of black hair, his beautiful eyes — richly and transparently amber-brown — shone with a light that had never been in them before. The Lady and her sisters saw it with a pang and knew that indeed the moment had come, the path must be taken.

'Your cousins,' repeated the Lady, smiling, yet with a melancholy air. 'Lionel and Bors are their names.'

'Lionel and Bors …' echoed Lancelot.

'They too have been orphaned, and so, until the time is right, they are to be with you here. You will all be taught together, and we will have to make sure that …'

But Lancelot had stopped listening. He was staring at the doorway, where two strangers had appeared: two boys, one about his own age and his own build too, tall and thin, with a long, pale, anxious face; the other smaller and younger, with a round-cheeked face that should have been merry but looked woebegone at the moment. They stared back at him; and the Lady and her sisters, watching them, could not help smiling.

'Come in, Lionel and Bors,' said the Lady.

Lancelot saw that his cousins' faces were filled with an unease that was close to fear. He could not understand why, exactly. But this was his home, he thought; it was up to him to make them feel comfortable. And so he walked towards them, hands held out.

'Welcome to the Lake, my cousins,' he said. 'You are most welcome. Most welcome.'

The two boys watched him warily. They held out their hands a little reluctantly and clasped his briefly, then withdrew them again. Lancelot saw that the smaller boy's brown eyes were rimmed with red, and that the tall boy looked very weary. 'Don't be afraid,' he whispered. 'You will be well here, and happy. We —'

To his horror, the smaller boy burst into loud sobbing, and his brother clumsily tried to comfort him, patting his shoulder and murmuring. Lancelot hesitated, then blurted out, 'I am sorry if I have hurt you, but I thought that you might —'

'Lancelot,' said the Lady gently, 'will you take Lionel and Bors to the room we have prepared for them? It is just by yours,' she added, as Lancelot looked questioningly at her. 'You can show them around the Lake afterwards.'

Lancelot was disturbed. This was such a strange, such a new experience for him, yet he wanted so much to make the boys feel welcome. But already he had managed to frighten the younger one into tears. He looked questioningly at the Lady. Her gaze back at him was limpid and inscrutable as the waters of the Lake. She was not going to tell him how to do it.

'Come with me, then,' he said uncertainly, darting a glance at the younger boy to see if he would burst into tears again at the sound of his voice. But the child just sniffed and wiped his nose on his sleeve, while his brother, pink with embarrassment, nodded. So Lancelot led the way out of the dining hall, towards the bedchambers.

Cousins! They were his cousins! And definitely human — not of the Lake. For the first time, the reality of being a human person and not an Otherworlder like the Lakelanders, struck him. The boys were not perfectly beautiful, perfectly formed, gliding and graceful, as were the ladies of the Lake and their servants. Neither were they the diversity of shapes and forms of the creatures of the Lake, or the world above the water. They were like himself — gawky and unfinished. Where had they come from, his cousins?

He had fallen silent, sunk in his thoughts, and was startled when the younger boy said, with a giggle, 'You looked just like an owl, just now, did you know? I didn't know we were cousins to an owl!'

'Don't be silly, Bors,' said Lionel a trifle anxiously, looking sideways at Lancelot, who was rather puzzled by Bors' quick change from damp misery to bright sunshine.

'An owl?' he replied. 'I have heard of them. Not seen them. They have round eyes, don't they? And they are very wise. Not like me at all.'

Bors laughed frankly now, and this time, Lionel joined in, rather more discreetly. 'Have you never really seen an owl?' Lionel said at last. 'In the woods?'

'The woods?' said Lancelot.

Bors and Lionel looked at each other. Lancelot flushed a little. 'Woods I have not seen. Except in books.'

'What about castles?' said Bors.

'Cities?' said Lionel.

'Warhorses?' said Bors.

'Tournaments?' said Lionel.

'Orchards?' said Bors.

'Stables?' said Lionel.

'Stop, stop.' Lancelot held up a hand. 'All these things I know about, you understand, because there are books here about them, but I have never seen them.'

The boys looked at him pityingly. Lancelot, sensing the pity, said proudly, 'But I know the Lake, with its deep, peaceful halls, full of beauty and contentment. I know the waters of the Lake, of jewel brightness and clarity. I know the world-above-the-water, with sand

and dunes and the roar of the ocean, and all the birds and the insects that live there, and the wild briny smell of the ocean, and the oysters, hiding their pearls on the rocks. This has been my home for many, many years, and I love it dearly.'

Lionel burst out, 'But you really come from another world, Lancelot! Another home, which was destroyed by the Lake! Your father was King Ban of Benuic, and your mother Queen Elaine. Their stronghold was up there, in that place you call the world-above-the-water. Once there was a thriving town there, with many people, and a big castle, set between two waters, between the Lake and the Ocean. One day, when you were a baby, a terrible storm arose, a storm that seemed not quite natural. The sea rose hugely, in enormous waves, and the Lake rose too, and the two waters came roaring and screaming down upon the town. It was completely engulfed, and nothing and no-one survived, or so we thought — until today. What had once been a bustling, busy town became a wasteland of sand and water.'

Lancelot could hardly breathe. His chest hurt. A pain greater than any he had ever known was tearing at him. Then everything he had known, all the love and peace and gentleness, had that been a false thing too? Lionel had said the storm was no natural thing. Had — oh, terrible thought — had the Lady of the Lake caused it to happen, with all her magic?

'Lancelot,' said the voice of the Lady, suddenly at his shoulder. 'Lancelot, that is not the way to the right place.' Her voice was as sweet and as soft as ever, but he feared her, suddenly. Lionel and Bors were also taken aback by her sudden appearance, and her quiet words; a flush had spread over Lionel's pale face, and Bors was biting on his lip.

'Well, Lancelot?' she went on. 'Do you know the right place where you must go?'

'My Lady,' said Lancelot, holding himself straight, though he melted with angry fear inside, 'I think I do know it now. And it is not here.'

'No,' she said sadly. 'It is not. But for a while yet, it must be.' She looked at Lancelot for an instant more, then at Lionel and Bors. 'My poor children,' she said softly, 'you have been taught to fear the Lake, and so I cannot blame you. But for the moment, your home is here too.' Her eyes glittered and her mouth set in a firm line. 'And tomorrow, you start your lessons. But first, Lancelot, I will see you in the dining hall, after you have escorted your cousins to their chambers.'

'Yes, my Lady,' said Lancelot. When she had gone, he led the other two boys to the chamber that was to be theirs. He could not speak, even when Lionel and Bors timidly said they would see him later, but only nodded, his stomach churning.

The Lady was waiting for him. She was alone. She motioned him to rise when he knelt before her. She made him sit beside her and looked at him for a long time. Lancelot tried to evade the depths of that gaze; the new knowledge surging inside him, the old certainties wavering, and in between, a wasteland of confusion and sadness and rage and fear. She sighed and bade him give her his hand. In her own hand was a ring. A silver ring, perfectly plain, but bright and thin as a sliver of moon.

'Lancelot,' she said, 'this is yours. I have been waiting for the right time to give it to you.' She slipped the ring on his finger. 'It will protect you from false enchantments and help you to see truly. You will always be under the protection of the Lake. But in a year's time, you must leave here and return to the human world. You, and your cousins. You will have learnt everything that we here can teach you, and will need to learn the ways of men, and especially of knights. You will become a great knight, Lancelot, one day. And in that year, Lionel and Bors will learn some of the ways of the Lake, for they need to.'

Lancelot had been silent until then, but he could contain himself no longer. The ring burning on his finger like a cold star, the red pain aching in his stomach, the passion bursting in his head and his heart: they goaded him into a very great daring. 'You speak of a future to me,' he said harshly, 'yet you stole my past. Why should my cousins learn the ways of the Lake, which destroyed all that should have been mine?'

The Lady's eyes flashed angrily, but all she said was, 'You are still a child, Lancelot.'

The wildness surged in him, at her words. 'I am not! Not any more!' Swallowing, he went on. 'My parents … they died … because of …'

'They died,' she finished for him quietly. 'Storms come; people build on shifting sands, and the sea engulfs them.'

'But the waters of the Lake rose too, and —'

'Lionel and Bors told you that. But they know nothing. Less than nothing. They have been told stories by people who know nothing except for fear and lack of understanding. It has been thus for a long time. But soon, the time draws near when at last the Lake and the world of men will be linked again; through you, and others like you. Yes, Lancelot, there was once a town up there on the sands; yes, your family lived there; yes, a storm came and took it away; yes, we rescued you and brought you up in the Lake. We did so because we had to, Lancelot; because you were needed, important, in the work that was to come. We could no more cause that storm than stop it.'

'My parents,' said Lancelot, pale as death. 'Why did you not save them too?'

The Lady's lovely face went very still. 'It was almost more than we could do, saving you, my poor child,' she said gently. 'Our magic is strong, but not against the sea. We risked being swept away ourselves. They,

Ban and Elaine, were already dead when we rescued you. But your mother … it was your mother Elaine who pleaded with us to save you. Did you not hear her voice, in your dream of the storm?'

He could hear her voice now, hear the words clearly. 'Lancelot, Lancelot,' she had called, had screamed; not in fear, then, but in pleading, in desperate entreaty, to save him. And the Lady of the Lake had come.

Lancelot bowed his head. 'Forgive me,' he said brokenly. 'I should have known, all these years I've been here, that never could … never could this place be associated with evil, and betrayal, and wicked magic.'

'Why shouldn't you doubt us?' said the Lady. 'We have not told you, in all this time. But that was to protect you. One day, Lancelot, you will understand why.'

'I wish …' said Lancelot, and then he stopped. The Lady waited, almost anxiously, he thought, suddenly, strangely. But the family of the Lake were never anxious. 'Lady,' he went on in a rush, 'Lady, you said I was important, and thus must be saved, though indeed I do not understand why that should be. But, afterwards, was it …?'

The Lady smiled suddenly, and her smile held an odd mixture of desolation and joy. 'Was it for love we kept you, fed you, tended you, taught you, made you our own? Was it for love that the Lake made Lancelot? Is that what you want to know?'

'Yes,' he said simply.

'It was for love indeed,' said the Lady. 'We knew we must lose you, one day. But love is your gift. You gave it to us. We could not refuse it. We *would* not,' she added fiercely.

Lancelot stared at her, overcome. He did not yet know his own nature, and his own magic. He looked down at his hand, where the ring glowed, and he whispered, 'Thank you. I … I … cannot find any —'

'I think perhaps it is too early to rest,' the Lady said, her voice suddenly brisk and bright. 'Go and get your cousins, tell them there's a feast on. It's never too early for them to learn about the Lake.'

Lancelot smiled. 'They won't be resting,' he said. 'They'll be wide awake, whispering; or staring at the walls and scared.'

'Don't be too sure, with human children,' said the Lady. 'You were asleep as soon as we took you from that storm.'

For an instant Lancelot's heart lurched again, as the pictures of the past fell into his mind; but he said, almost steadily, 'They said it was a wasteland, the world-above-the-water; but it is not. It is a beautiful place, and will one day be filled with the sound of human voices as well. I will build a castle there, one day, in memory of my parents; and call it Joyous Gard.'

The Lady's face had stilled again. 'One day, you will, my dear Lancelot. But not yet. For now, for another year, you are of the Lake.'

'I am of the Lake!' agreed Lancelot happily, and went off to rouse his cousins.

AUTHOR'S NOTE

When I was a child, my father would tell us stories of the place near Bordeaux where his grandmother had a house, called Soulac, in the Medoc (the name Medoc comes from a Latin phrase meaning 'between two waters'). Soulac, which these days is a beautiful resort town, is on the very tip of a peninsula that juts out between the Atlantic Ocean and the Gironde River, where the river is so huge it resembles a lake.

My great-grandmother's house was swept away by the sea in the 1940s, only one of a series of incidents over the centuries that saw Soulac constantly rebuilt as a result of incursions by the sands and the sea, and many legends of underwater bells and so on.

We speculated about the name of the place: 'Soulac' is very close to the French phrase 'sous le lac', or under the lake. But it was only recently that I learnt Soulac, at the time situated on an island, had once been a bustling Roman town. In the sixth century, a huge storm arose and swept the entire town away. When the tides retreated, the sands took over and the deserted spot eventually became a peninsula. Slowly, it was repopulated. In the twelfth century, a beautiful church called Notre Dame de la Fin des Terres, or Our Lady of Land's End, was built — but again the sea and sands intervened, burying the church and the little settlement around it under the dunes. It was only rediscovered in the nineteenth century.

Soulac seemed the perfect setting for Lancelot's childhood, and for the sense of his mysterious past that is never fully explained in the legend, but which still seems to hang over him. In keeping with this, I have used as my base the French rather than English traditions about him. For Lancelot first makes his appearance in the Arthurian legend in the twelfth-century French narrative poem by Chretien de Troyes, 'Le Chevalier de la Charette', or The Knight of the Cart. And so the legend of the greatest, the most tragic, the most beautiful and mysterious of the knights of the Round Table began.

ISEULT

Richard Harland

'Look what I've done!'

Iseult came rushing into the cottage, eyes alight and hair streaming out behind. In her arms she cradled a small dog with white and tan markings. Urtha was busy grinding herbs for one of her potions. Grumpy as ever, she didn't turn round straightaway.

'He was dying of poison berries. I found him under a bush by the pool of St Nicholas. There was froth coming out of his mouth, horrible grey froth.'

Finally Urtha turned. 'What did you do?'

'All the things you taught me. I squeezed the

149

juice of nettle stalks and trickled it down his throat. I made him eat some ragwort and primrose flowers.'

'And the incantations?'

'Yes, I said them all. I *willed* him better! I'm a real healer now! Aren't you proud of me?'

Urtha examined the dog. 'He seems in very good health. What time did you say you found him?'

Iseult dropped her eyes. 'Just after breakfast.'

'Four hours ago? Why didn't you bring him to me?'

'I wanted to do it by myself. I wanted to prove how much I've learned.'

'Hmph. I wondered where you were all morning.'

Getting praise out of Urtha was like getting blood out of a stone. Iseult thought of her as a gruff old gnome. So short and stumpy, with bristling black eyebrows and iron-grey hair. And living in this lonely cottage a mile out from town. Surely, with her skills and knowledge, she should have been a person of importance?

'I want to take him to my father's court,' said Iseult. 'I want to show them my first cured patient.'

Urtha looked at her for a long moment before speaking. 'Do you, indeed? But there are more important things than pleasing fathers. Even if they are the King of Ireland.'

Here it comes, thought Iseult. Another lecture on the sanctity of the healer's calling. But instead Urtha shrugged, with a hint of a smile pulling at the corners of her mouth.

'Very well. Be off with you.'

Iseult didn't get to see her father, because something happened first. On her way to his private chambers, she passed through the Great Hall. The ladies of the castle were directing the servants, arranging tables and decorations for the Feast of Swithin. Iseult hadn't attended a feast in all the three months she'd been living and training with Urtha.

She couldn't resist the urge to boast.

'Look what I did! I healed this dog when he was almost dead!' She held out the dog. 'I brought him back to life!'

The ladies left their tasks and gathered around.

'What a darling puppy,' said one.

'I've seen those markings somewhere before,' said another.

'Who does he belong to?' asked a third.

Iseult's heart sank with sudden foreboding.

'Nobody.' She stuck out her chin. 'I saved him. He's mine.'

But in the next moment, her foreboding was fulfilled.

'Darassy!' shrilled a voice. 'My Darassy!'

It was Fayence, recently married to Morholt, the king's champion. She was tall and thin like a pale waterbird. Though six years older than Iseult, she had a childish manner and a childish voice.

Fayence rushed forward with outstretched arms, but Iseult clutched the dog to her chest.

'He's not your Darassy. What was he doing by the pool of St Nicholas, if he's yours?'

'He ran away two days ago.' Fayence pointed. 'See how he knows me? See how he's looking at me?'

Iseult squeezed the dog so that it changed position in her arms. 'He's not looking at you now.'

'Darassy!' Feyence called in a wheedling tone. 'Darassy! Darassy! Darassy!'

'Stop calling him that!'

'Who is he then?'

'He's … he's … Tomlin. That's his name, Tomlin.'

'Liar!' Fayence began to shriek at the top of her voice. 'Give him to me!'

Iseult answered her glare for glare. Her fierce intensity was more than a match for Fayence's childish temper. Then she spun scornfully on her heel and marched out of the hall with the dog in her arms.

The next morning, King Anguish himself paid a visit to Urtha's cottage. The wise woman had gone out on her rounds to tend the sick and bedridden. Iseult was alone when her father arrived.

She had already made preparations. She had guessed that the scene in the hall would have repercussions. The dog was hidden out of sight, tied up to a tree in the wood behind the cottage.

Her father had his usual careworn look. He wore gold rings and a rich red robe, but there was no sparkle in his personality.

'This business with the dog,' he began.

'He must have gone off somewhere,' said Iseult innocently.

'This business with the dog,' King Anguish repeated. 'I don't think you understand what it means, Iseult. Fayence has been complaining to Morholt. And Morholt has been complaining to me.'

'So? You're the king, aren't you?'

'A king is only as strong as his supporters. Morholt is my champion and my greatest weapon of war. Without him, it would be difficult to extract a tribute from the Cornish duchies.'

Iseult sniffed. 'Money and calculations,' she muttered under her breath.

'What was that?'

'I was only saying, I'm your daughter. Don't my feelings matter?'

'Iseult, you're my favourite daughter, and I indulge you in too many ways already. Even this whim to be trained as a healer. But I will *not* offend Morholt unnecessarily.' His eyes flashed with sudden irritation. 'Damn it all, it's only a dog!'

'My dog! I saved his life! I have a right to him!'

King Anguish shook his head. His irritation had changed to a kind of weary inflexibility.

'I want that dog returned to Fayence today. Bring it to the castle and hand it over before nightfall. Or else.'

'Or else what?'

But King Anguish didn't need to reply. Iseult knew the *or else*. Her training as a healer would be at an end and she would be married off as her sisters had been married off.

She watched her father's retreating back as he left the cottage and headed for his horse. There was no way out. She was in an impossible position.

She went straight to the dog in the wood. When she untied him, he wanted to play, but Iseult lay down on the soft green moss at the base of the tree. She turned him over on his side and wrapped herself round him.

There was a clenched feeling in the pit of her stomach. How could she bear to give him up? How could she bear to let Fayence have him? That overgrown girl only wanted him as a toy. Fayence was too shallow to care deeply about anything.

Her eyes wandered over his coat and markings. Such lovely little patches of tan on white. He really was the most beautiful dog! She'd never realised quite how special he was before.

She traced out the markings with her index finger. The dog nuzzled and pretended to bite at the finger. Iseult took his head between her hands and quietened him down with soothing noises.

'Tomlin, Tomlin, Tomlin,' she murmured. 'Tomlin, Tomlin, Tomlin.'

She said it a hundred times over. With every repetition, she felt she was planting the name deeper into his mind. Not Fayence's Darassy, but *her* Tomlin. Her very own Tomlin.

She began to sketch out a kind of daydream about him. What if she did hand him over, but he wouldn't stay with Fayence? Even if Fayence kept him locked up, however long she kept him locked up? Still his one and only wish would be to return to the person who really loved him. And sooner or later, he would manage to escape …

She brought her face up close to his muzzle and looked into his eyes.

'Tomlin, I love you,' she said. 'I'd do anything to have you with me. You know that, don't you?'

The dog shifted and blinked. She couldn't interpret the expression in his eyes. She would have liked to believe it was love, but she couldn't be sure.

Then an idea came into her mind, an idea so extraordinary that she gasped out loud.

A love potion!

Only a week ago, an old miller from Esling had come asking Urtha for a love potion to use on his young wife. Urtha had refused, but not because she didn't have the ingredients. Iseult was sure she had the ingredients, and the recipe too. It would be in her leather-bound volume of secret lore.

Iseult snapped her fingers and jumped to her feet. If she could find the recipe, she could make up the potion herself. When Tomlin drank it, he would *have* to return to her!

She gathered the dog in her arms. How long before Urtha came home? She would need to move very fast.

It didn't take her long to find the recipe. She didn't know if the potion would work on a dog, or what size of dose Tomlin would need. She decided to make up the same dose as for a human being.

She mashed, strained, brewed and decanted. The dog frisked around the kitchen, excited by the frantic activity.

'Keep out of the way, Tomlin,' said Iseult sharply, after she'd nearly tripped over him for the third time. 'I'm doing this for you.'

She couldn't be sure about all the ingredients. Urtha kept many of her herbs and infusions in unmarked bottles. Iseult had to trust her memory as best she could.

Finally it was ready: half a cupful of thin yellowish

liquid. It looked unpleasant and smelled bitter. She doubted whether Tomlin would lap it up from a bowl. She would have to disguise it in food.

When she looked around, though, the dog was nowhere to be seen. The back door of the cottage was shut, but the door to the parlour was open. She went through and discovered that the front door was also open. Had Urtha not closed it properly when she went out on her rounds?

Iseult stood on the threshold and called Tomlin's name. In vain. She could have wept with frustration. What a perverse time to go wandering!

Then a terrible thought struck her. What if he'd gone wandering back to the castle? What if he'd gone wandering back to Fayence?

The mere possibility gave her a physical pain in the chest. She remembered how she'd taken him over the route yesterday. If he'd been lost before, he knew the way now. He knew the way back to his old mistress.

But surely he wouldn't, or would he? She could no longer tell what was possible or impossible. The thought of Fayence fussing over her Tomlin drove her mad.

She had to find out! She set off running towards the castle.

She had no idea what she would do. But she would do something. She wouldn't let it happen. Never, never, never!

She rushed into the Great Hall shouting, 'Where's Fayence?' Soldiers and retainers sat at the long tables, lords and ladies sat at the high table. All around was a hubbub of laughter and conversation. Many were already breaking bread and raising their goblets. But the meat had not yet been served. They were waiting for King Anguish, whose chair was still empty.

Iseult darted between benches up to the high table. There was Fayence! She was chattering like a parrot to Morholt, her husband.

She stopped chattering when she saw Iseult. A kind of sneer passed over her face. Iseult needed no further proof.

'What have you done with him?' Iseult yelled. 'Where is he?'

Fayence knew immediately what she was talking about. 'You tell me!' she yelled back.

'Don't bait her, Fayence,' said Morholt, frowning. 'You have what you wanted.'

'Does she?' Iseult leaned forward across the table. 'But not for long! I'll … I'll …'

Too angry for words, she swept out and struck a goblet of wine. Red drops went flying over Fayence's embroidered gown.

Morholt's frown deepened. 'This is no way …'

But Fayence had already jumped to her feet. 'She

hasn't brought him! She was supposed to bring him! By nightfall, the king said! He said it was an order! Where's my Darassy?'

'You've got him,' Iseult charged.

'No, you have!'

Iseult shook her head. 'He ran away to you.' But she was no longer so sure of herself.

'Excuses! Excuses!' shrilled Fayence. Everyone in the hall was staring now. 'You're trying to blame me so you don't have to obey! It was an order!' She turned to her husband. 'Make her fetch my dog!'

'That's for the king to do,' answered Morholt.

Fayence was flushed and panting. Suddenly she snatched up a knife from the table and brandished it in Iseult's direction.

'Fetch him! Now, now, now!'

Morholt put out a hand to check her. But Fayence was beyond control. She launched herself across the table and slashed with the knife.

Iseult gaped at the blood streaming from her arm. She grabbed at the hand that held the knife. Her hatred lent her strength. She dragged Fayence across the table and wrestled her to the ground.

There was uproar in the hall, but no-one was close enough to separate them. They rolled over and over across the floor.

Fayence managed to bring her other hand round for a second grip on the knife-handle. Iseult's gashed arm was numb and useless. Fayence rose up on her elbows and forced the blade towards Iseult's chest.

'Hold!' commanded a loud authoritative voice. 'Hold, both of you!'

It was King Anguish, entering the hall. At his side was Urtha, the wise woman.

Fayence and Iseult returned to their senses. They let go of the knife as if it had become suddenly red hot and it clattered to the floor. They sat up side by side, like naughty children. Blood continued to trickle from the deep gash in Iseult's arm.

Urtha was like a small black thundercloud. She didn't wait for the king's permission to speak.

'You fools! Look at you! Over a dog!'

'My Darassy,' pouted Fayence.

'My Tomlin,' muttered Iseult.

The thundercloud approached and stood over them. 'Not your anything. A dog isn't a possession like a dress or a ring.'

Iseult made a sudden leap of realisation. 'You took him!'

'Yes, I took him. I came home and saw you through the kitchen window. I watched what you were doing. You were trying to concoct a love potion.'

Fayence let out an 'Oh!' of indignation. Iseult's cheeks burned with embarrassment.

'I came secretly into the parlour and called the dog away. I brought the poor thing here to your father.'

'You were trying to avoid my order, Iseult,' said King Anguish.

'I intended to hand him over,' said Iseult miserably.

'False obedience!' snapped Urtha. 'You intended him to come running back to you. I know what the love potion was for. How could you be so cruel and stupid?'

'Cruel? Stupid?'

'Yes. To use a human love potion on an animal. Haven't I told you a hundred times that the medicine has to be appropriate to the patient? You could've killed him. You would've killed him.'

Iseult shook her head. She didn't want to hear. But Urtha went on remorselessly.

'I watched what you were doing, Iseult. You were guessing at ingredients. You didn't know what was in the unmarked jars. One of the herbs you mixed in was Roscommon Wort. It produces violent spasms, nothing to do with a love potion.'

Fayence looked at Iseult with shocked, accusing eyes. 'You wanted to kill him so I couldn't have him!'

'No,' said Urtha. 'She didn't want to kill him. She just didn't want to think about what she was doing. She let her emotions blind her to the risk.' Urtha stamped her foot on the floor in front of Iseult. 'What were the chances that he'd die, do you think?'

'I don't know.'

'Think!'

'I suppose … I suppose it was an even chance that he'd live or die.'

'Yes, Iseult. An even chance. You claim to love this dog, but how much do you really care for him? He dies for your love. What sort of a love is that?'

'But I'd have …' Iseult's voice faded away.

She was about to say she'd have been willing to die for Tomlin too. But suddenly it seemed a silly thing to say about a dog.

She hung her head. But a cry from Fayence made her look up.

'There he is, there he is!'

The dog had just been carried into the hall, under the arm of one of the king's stewards. Fayence bubbled over with delight.

'Bring him to me!'

'No,' said Urtha and King Anguish in the very same moment.

The king gestured towards Iseult's bleeding arm.

'There has been enough trouble over this dog already,' he said. 'You have both behaved improperly. Therefore neither of you shall have the dog.'

Fayence's mouth crinkled pettishly. 'That's not fair.'

'It would not be fair to the dog to have either of you as his mistress. Even a dog deserves better than that.' King Anguish signalled to the steward. 'I shall ask Urtha to take him and give him as a gift to the first shepherd boy she meets.'

'A shepherd boy?' Fayence was horrified.

King Anguish made no reply. The steward passed the dog across into Urtha's arms.

There was silence in the hall as Urtha stomped off towards the door. Then she halted and lowered the dog to the ground.

'And get that wounded arm fixed up immediately,' she ordered over her shoulder.

She gave a low whistle and the dog followed her out through the door.

Iseult returned to the cottage with her arm tightly bandaged. It was late at night, but a candle still burned in the parlour. Iseult had deliberately taken her time, hoping to get back after Urtha had gone to bed. No such luck!

The wise woman was sitting at a low wooden table. She had set out four bowls of water and drawn a pattern of lines on the table-top. She appeared more serious than angry.

Iseult didn't ask about the dog. One look at Urtha's face told her that the king's order had been carried out to the letter. In a strange way, it didn't seem to matter much any more. She felt as though a storm had washed over her and passed on.

'Do you know what I've been doing, Iseult?'

'Scrying?'

'Yes. Seeking a glimpse of the future. Your future.'

Now Iseult noticed the objects placed between the lines on the table-top. Her own tortoiseshell comb, a piece of paper with her handwriting, some strands of dark red hair. She was instantly curious.

'What did you see? Will I become a great healer?'

'Yes. But that's not what you'll be famous for.'

'I'm going to be famous?'

'Famous for love. For your passion towards one particular man. They'll make up stories about the two of you.'

'Who is he?'

'I can't tell.'

'Will he love me back? As much as I love him?'

'Yes.'

Iseult grinned a fierce kind of grin. 'That's all I want.'

Urtha shook her head sadly. 'It won't have a happy ending, Iseult. It won't be a happy love affair.'

'Why? Is he going to die?'

Urtha spread her arms. Either she didn't know or she wouldn't say.

'Am I going to die?'

Still no answer. Iseult thought for a moment. When she raised her head, her eyes were wet, but her chin was firm and determined.

'I don't care about a happy ending,' she said. 'As long as I have the love.'

AUTHOR'S NOTE

The story of Tristan and Iseult (or Tristran and Ysolt, or Tristram and Isolde) has always had a special fascination for me. It's so unusual for medieval times — an irresistible love affair outside of marriage, where you can't help cheering on the lovers completely against morality, against social duty, even against the obligations of friendship. And the ending never fails to move me: when Tristan, wounded and dying, can only be saved if Iseult (who has indeed become a great healer) manages to come to him in time. A ship approaches, which will have white sails if it bears Iseult. But Tristan's legal wife falsely tells him that it has black sails. Tristan dies in despair, and Iseult, when she lands and hears the news, dies of grief.

The story started out as an independent tale, but later joined up with the Arthurian cycle. Tristan and Iseult even stayed for a while in Camelot.

Surely this has to be the first and greatest tragedy of love! Romeo and Juliet, eat your hearts out!

PERCIVAL

Ursula Dubosarsky

erry could never remember a time when he hadn't lived in the small house in the forest. Nor could he remember a time when he hadn't been called Perry, although he knew his name was Percival. It was written in his mother's passport which he had found one day while looking for drawing paper at the very bottom of her wooden filing cabinet, while she was lying with her eyes closed in the garden listening to birds.

He had discovered his own name and something more in the little hard black booklet with the gold writing and the mysterious word, 'Passport' written on the cover. Inside was a photograph of his mother, and the names of her children. Three children — himself, Percival, with his date of birth — and then two older brothers he never knew he had. His mother's passport included them all — those were the days when children were not required to have their own documents but could be attached to their mother, like suckling piglets. Himself, Percival, six months, his brother Brun, four years and eight months, and his other brother Derek, nine years and one month.

He should perhaps have been more shocked than he was. Brothers, two brothers, he had never heard of. But for Perry it was more in the nature of a confirmation of secrets. His mother smelt of endless secrets, and his brothers were only another of them. He put the passport back under all the papers where he had found it.

Perry and his mother lived alone, with a tall turbaned man named Rajiv. Rajiv wore a turban because he was a Sikh, which meant he had never cut his hair, not once in his life, but rolled it up and hid it underneath the long shiny cloth. Perry had never seen Rajiv's hair because he only removed the turban just before he climbed into bed with Perry's mother at night, and the door was always closed and there was no keyhole.

Rajiv was not his father. Perry did not know where his father was. He had asked his mother, long before the coming of Rajiv.

'Where is my daddy?'

He knew from the books his mother read to him that children had mothers and fathers.

'He was lost,' was all his mother said, and that was all she ever said.

Lost. And now he also knew he had two lost brothers as well. How had his mother lost them all?

Perry told Rajiv about his father the first morning Rajiv came to live with them. They were sitting at the table eating sandwiches. His mother was in the shower.

'My father was lost, you know.'

Rajiv looked at him sideways.

'When a man goes out into the forest in the morning,' replied Rajiv, 'and comes home in the evening, we do not call him a lost man.'

Rajiv often spoke like this, using the word *we*. Perry was never quite sure who he meant, or what he meant for that matter and this first exchange was no exception. Did he mean that Perry's father was going to come home one evening to their little cottage? Perry found himself looking out the window at night, wondering if it was true.

They lived in a strange seclusion, Perry, his mother and Rajiv, deep in the shadows of a pine forest, in a house made of sandstone and rotting wood. Only one road led out of the forest, just a walking track, scarcely wide enough for a bicycle. Every few days his mother or Rajiv walked the track to the village shops to buy food and paper and clothes. They did not have to go to work. His mother had plenty of money.

When he was small, before Rajiv, she carried him with her down the track, first in her arms, then on her back. Perry could remember it, just. He enjoyed it, he pretended she was a horse. He remembered the tension in her body, as though she was on guard for a predator. Then as he grew bigger, she began to leave him in the house alone. He was safe enough. He would not wander off alone, and no-one came into the forest.

Perry did not go to school. Rajiv taught him to read and to do simple sums. That was why Rajiv had come to live with them.

'I can't teach you,' was his mother's explanation.

'Why not?'

'I can't teach anyone anything,' said his mother. 'I can't make anyone do anything.'

'But why can't I go to school?' Perry said.

He knew there were schools the same way he knew there were fathers, from books. They did not have a television or a computer, but they had books. His mother ordered them specially, carefully chosen. When he was older, Perry realised how very carefully chosen those books had been.

'Rajiv will teach you,' said his mother.

So Rajiv taught him, words in the morning and numbers in the afternoon. Perry enjoyed learning things. But Rajiv was not happy, Perry could tell. He would look at Perry and frown and then raise his dark eyes to the ceiling.

One day Rajiv banged down the pencil on the table and said to Perry's mother, 'The boy must see other children. It's not right. He must play with boys his own age.'

A strange trembling look came over his mother's face. She grasped Rajiv's beautiful long hands together, as though she were praying to him. But he shook his head.

'He must,' said Rajiv. 'For his sake.'

Perry had never seen another child. For him they were creatures in books, as mythical as dragons.

Not long after that, Rajiv went out one morning, his golden turban glinting in the scraps of sun that shone through the pine branches, and came back with two boys, one on each side of him. They were twins, and they had come to play.

Perry was frightened and fascinated at the same time. He could not stop looking at them. How small they were, just like him, with soft skin and shining hair.

Rajiv and his mother went out into the garden and left the children alone to play.

'Where are your toys?' said the boys, looking around them.

Perry took the twins into his room. They stared at the shelves of puzzles, building blocks, teddy bears and texta colours.

'Where are your cars?' said the boys.

'What?' said Perry.

'Your toy cars. Where are your toy cars?'

Perry said nothing; he didn't know what to say. Soon the boys found the box of puppets and the toy stage. They lay on the floor making marvellous noises and waving their arms and legs about.

Then Rajiv came back inside. He made the children jam sandwiches and then took the boys away, one on each side of him down the path the way they had come.

'What are cars?' Perry asked his mother after Rajiv had taken the twins away.

His mother had stared, speechless for a moment. Then she knelt down next to him and pinched his arm very hard.

'Never, never say that word,' she whispered. 'Never, never.'

After that, Rajiv and his mother began to fight. Looking back, it seemed to Perry that up until that time they had lived together in a mysterious peace, like angels in heaven. But after the twins came the spell was broken. Doors were slammed, voices became loud and angry, things were thrown. His mother cried. Rajiv cried too, huge dewy tears. He wiped them carefully from his cheeks and mouth with a silken handkerchief.

It was on the occasion of such a quarrel that Perry slipped out the back door by himself. It was early in the evening in summer, the sun was just starting to set but it would be light for some time yet. He ran out to the end of the garden and hid himself behind a crop of tall tomato vines. At this distance, the sound of the angry voices from the cottage were muffled and became almost musical. The words disappeared into the air and the green leaves.

Perry closed his eyes. He started not to hear the voices, but instead cicadas and birds whistling and the rustle of pines. He felt tired and sad.

Then he started, as though jolted from sleep. He opened his eyes. What was that? In the distance, far away from the house there was a strange whirring rumble, a sound he had never heard before.

Perry got to his feet, listening intently. He heart was beating with an odd excitement. The rumble rose to a height, then died down, then rose to a height again. What was it?

Perry looked back to the cottage. The curtains were drawn. They had stopped fighting. But it would be a while before they remembered him again. He was not allowed to leave the end of the garden. Indeed, apart from those village trips so long ago on his mother's back, he never had. But that sound, he had to know the meaning of that sound!

He found his feet began walking away as if by themselves. His pace was quick, down that winding path. He broke into a run and ran through the forest.

The sound became louder, rising and falling relentlessly, humming, whirring, rumbling.

He reached the edge of the forest and stood still for a moment, panting. In front of him was the village shop. Its doors were closed. There were a few houses surrounding it, but they looked deserted.

The noise was very loud now, fiercer and stronger, like a wild lion, thought Perry, or a bear. He looked in the direction it seemed to be coming from. Over past the village shop was a line of tall trees. It must be coming from beyond there.

He ran to the green curtaining thickness of the trees. Now there was a smell as well as the sound, a smell of burning smoke and something else, an odour unlike anything he knew. It was not his mother's perfume or flowers or growing vegetables or the thick cottony smell of Rajiv's turban. This was bitter, wonderful. He breathed it in and felt strong and extraordinary.

He came up to the line of trees and moved through it, pushing his way past the branches. He stood behind a trunk of a very tall tree and looked.

There before him in a clear field was a circle, like the path through the forest, but leading nowhere, just round back on itself. Clouds of brown and black dust rose up from it. Suddenly right by his head something flew by him, nearly knocking him to the ground in shock.

But his eyes stayed wide open. Under the dust, speeding round and around, was a kind of a seat on four big black wheels. On the seat, domed in glass, sat a helmeted man, his two gloved hands on a wheel. Round and around the circular track it flew, around and around faster than thoughts, louder than thunder.

Time passed, Perry had no idea how long. He stood motionless gazing at the speeding contraption. Round and round and round. It seemed to him like the wind or an earthquake, or a mountain moving by itself. He had never suspected the world could hold anything in it so very wonderful. It filled him up, the noise, the movement, the smell, the speed, it filled him right up.

Then it stopped. There was a screeching. The dust subsided. The wheels stopped spinning. Perry felt dizzy and slightly sick. What had happened? Why had it stopped? Why did it ever have to stop?

The helmeted man on the seat pushed back the dome. There was a deep hissing sound. He stood up from the seat, slowly in his great black boots. He wore a white suit covering his whole body. He was huge and hidden. With the boots, the gloves and the helmet, every part of his skin was covered.

Two other men whom Perry had not noticed before were now walking towards the wheeled seat. One of them had a bottle of water, and handed it to the man in the helmet.

The man removed his helmet and gloves, placing them gently on the ground next to him, and took the bottle. In the glowing sunset Perry saw his pale hair spring from his head like feathers. The man lifted the bottle in the air and let the water tumble over his face, in his eyes, his mouth. Then he tossed the bottle aside and laid himself down on the grass, his face turned to the sky.

The two other men were busy at the wheeled seat. They had things in their hands — rags, bars. Perry could hear them shouting to each other, asking questions, ordering each other about.

Perry could not stop himself. He stepped out from behind the tree and walked towards them. He stood on the edge of the circle and waited.

One of the men looked up and said, 'We've got an audience.'

Perry could not speak. The man smiled, his face was smeared with black.

'It's all right, kid,' he said. 'Don't be shy. Come and have a look.'

How hot it was, how strong that burning smell. Perry trembled. He stepped towards them, towards it. He came very close, as close as he dared.

'Big engine, isn't it?' said the man. He wiped sweat from his forehead with a rag.

Perry stared down into it, at the silver and black screws and bolts and containers and wires and springs and pieces of rubber. It was like seeing the centre, the secret of the universe, the inside of God's head.

'What is it?' he said hoarsely.

'What is it?' said the man. 'What do you mean, what is it?'

He laughed, and nodded over to the other man who was leaning on the back wheels. 'You'd think he'd never seen a car before.'

A car! So this was a car. Of course, this was a car, this power, this violence, this complexity. This was it. This was everything.

'You like racing cars, kid?' said the man. 'You want to drive racing cars when you grow up?'

Perry gulped. 'Can I … can I go around and around, very fast?' he said. 'Like him?' And he pointed at the man who had been wearing the helmet and was now lying flat on his back, all energy spent, his face to the setting sun.

The man laughed again. He slapped Perry's back and laughed and laughed.

'You'll need a bit of practice before you can drive like him,' he said. 'You know who that is?'

Perry shook his head. How would he know? He didn't know anything or anyone, only his mother and Rajiv. The man said something, a name. It had a strange sound he could not understand.

'He's just the most famous driver in the world,' said the man. 'That's all he is.'

It was nearly dark.

'Go home, kid,' said the man who had done all the talking. 'Before we get in trouble. Off you go. Go on.'

Perry didn't move.

'Go on,' said the man again. 'Go home. Get your dad to give you some driving lessons.'

Perry looked over at where the man they called the driver lay still in the darkness, his white suit gleaming, the helmet and gloves beside him.

Now he knew.

He knew. He knew that he, Perry, would wear a white suit, and a white helmet on his head. He, Perry, would wear huge gloves and black boots and he would sit in that seat above that sound and drive a racing car. Round and around in circles, faster than anyone in the whole world, faster than anyone ever born.

Perry turned. He did not look back. He did not need to now. He ran back through the line of trees, past the village shop to the edge of the forest, down the winding path, back past the tall tomato plants and tumbled into the cottage door.

His mother and Rajiv were in the kitchen. Rajiv was calmly chopping vegetables. His mother's hair was loose, she looked very beautiful. But he, Perry, was a different person.

'Mother!' he cried. 'I know who I am! I know what I'm going to be! I've seen a car! I'm going to be a racing car driver!'

Rajiv stopped cutting. He laid the knife down quietly. His mother sank her head on the table and laid her cheek on the wide silver blade.

Neither of them spoke. What had he said?

'Did you hear me?' He was shouting now. 'I went down to the village and I saw a car, a racing car! It was so fast, so strong! Why didn't you ever tell me about cars? A car is the most wonderful thing in the world!'

Rajiv reached out and touched his mother's hair. She pulled herself away. She looked up at Perry, her expression full of anger, almost as though she hated him. He stepped backwards, afraid.

She left the kitchen, without speaking. Rajiv kept his eyes to the floor and would not look at him. They both stayed still as they heard her in the bedroom, pulling open drawers.

She came back into the room with something in her hand.

'There!' she cried, thrusting it at him. 'You want to be a racing car driver? Take it! Take all of it! That is what remains of him. That's all that's left.'

Perry took it in his fingers, a small white dried flower in the shape of a heart, on the end of a rough piece of string.

'I don't understand, Mother,' he said, shaking his head and looking up at her. 'What is this?'

'It was your father's,' said his mother. She hissed at him. She looked like a spider, she had spider's eyes. 'Your father's lucky charm. He said it brought him luck. He was wearing it when he died, when he was killed, when he killed himself.'

Perry stared.

'Yes, that is what he was, what you want to be,' she said. 'A racing car driver. They said he was the greatest driver in the world. A champion. But he killed himself in his car, and my babies with him. My little boys.'

She sank to the floor on her knees, head in her hands.

'I thought if I kept you away,' she whispered, 'away from everything and everyone, away from cars, so you would never see one or hear of one, then I would keep you for myself, you would not go out and leave me and die.'

Rajiv left the room. He went right out the house. He did not close the front door, he just walked away.

'And he is as dead as them all. That is all it is for, for death.'

For death.

'I'm sorry, Mother,' said Perry simply. 'But that's what I want.'

'So did he,' replied his mother.

AUTHOR'S NOTE

This story came to me from a television interview I saw with the Formula One champion Jacques Villeneuve. He told the story of his upbringing, how his father, also a racing driver, had died on the track, and how his mother had tried to keep all knowledge and pleasure in car racing from him as a child. Then as a teenager, on a school trip, he had seen cars racing and immediately knew this was all he wanted to do, to live life on this kind of edge of death, as his father had. It immediately brought to my mind the story of Percival's own secluded childhood, after his father and brothers were killed as knights, and then discovering his own inevitable vocation when seeing knights one day passing by and realising this was all he wanted to be.

ELAINE, LILY MAID OF ASTOLAT

Felicity Pulman

T hrough her childhood, and for as long as she could remember, a shadowy presence had shared Elaine's dreams, walking with her through a vast red plain, a wasteland so dry and barren that Elaine thought she must be in hell. In her dreams she always tried to escape, to reclaim her will, her soul, her life, yet she seemed trapped as surely as if she was bound in chains.

Just lately, the shadow had begun to claim her waking hours as well, promising escape, promising freedom. Instinct kept Elaine silent. She knew her father and brothers would laugh if she told them, but she knew also that this silent presence was not of her imagining, conjured up out of loneliness and isolation. The shadow was growing stronger, while her dreams were so vivid and disturbing that nightly,

Elaine woke in a heart-lurching panic. If only her mother was still alive to calm her fears and talk her into serenity, into an acceptance of her fate. If only her mother was still alive, her fate would be different and she would be serene.

If only …

'Laine!' Her father's voice, calling her to duty. With a sigh, Laine jumped out of bed and looked out of the window, preparing herself to face another day, face the rest of her life. Heat. Dust. Flies. Boredom. Nothing to do, and nowhere to go, stuck on a property in the middle of nowhere, with only her father and younger brothers for company. Laine pulled a face as she looked out across the dry, scrubby paddock then up towards a band of cloud on the horizon. The air felt sticky with unshed rain. Perhaps at last, it was on its way?

Laine imagined an army of sullen black clouds on the march; violent cracks of thunder, zigzags of lightning unzipping the sky. Rain beating hot and hard against her skin. It was like that, sometimes. Once, so her grandpa had told her, it had rained so long and so hard that water had covered the paddocks and the family had to be evacuated by boat. The house, built on a small rise, had survived the deluge but they'd lost everything else and had to start all over again. Laine slitted her eyes against the sun's glare, seeing the parched earth turn to red mud; seeing the water rise and rise, smoking in the sun, wet lips licking the house.

'Laine! Where's our breakfast?' Hastily, Laine threw on a pair of shorts and a T-shirt. Her long fair hair felt damp and heavy as she brushed it back, looping and securing it with an elastic band to cool her neck. Barefoot, she skimmed into the kitchen, already a furnace from the heat of the fuel stove. Her father and brothers were at the table, waiting for her.

'Slept in, did you?' Her father was fiddling with the radio dial, trying to find a signal through the static.

'Sorry.' Laine forced a smile as she hastily dragged out boxes of cereal and long life milk. The family's working day started early, to make the most of the coolness of dawn. Her job was to have breakfast ready for her father and brothers when they came in, but a nightmare had kept her tossing uneasily in bed. She'd dreamt she was trapped in a tower that was entirely surrounded by water. Someone was with her, a shadowy presence who yearned for freedom even as Laine prayed that the water might rise high enough to drown them both. She had never felt such despair before, such a blackness of the soul.

'We're almost at the end of the feed.' Her father rubbed a brown, weather-beaten hand over the grey stubble on his chin. Worry lines creased his forehead as he continued. 'Reckon we've got a few days left, at most.'

'Then what?' Laine felt the blast of heat from the stove sucking her dry as she threw some sausages into a frypan.

Her father left the newsreader muttering quietly in the background while he turned his attention to his bowl of cornflakes. 'I'll have to drive the cattle up the track, hope I can find some grazing, keep them alive a little longer. Otherwise …' His slumped shoulders spoke of his despair.

'Will we have to move?' Laine felt ashamed of the joy she felt at the prospect of moving somewhere else. Anywhere but here.

Her father shrugged. 'No good going to the bank. They don't care that this property has been farmed for three generations. What would they know about drought and floods and fire? All they care about is balancing their bloody books.' He looked up, fierce and sullen. 'They're not forcing me into city life just yet,' he declared. 'I'll look elsewhere for a loan if they refuse me again.'

'Hurry up, Laine!' Eddie spooned up the last of his cereal and pushed his plate away.

'Make some toast while you're waiting.' Laine pulled a loaf from the freezer and set it in front of him. He looked at her blankly. 'Mum always had breakfast waiting for us when we came in,' he whined.

Biting back a response, Laine turned the sausages then prised a few slices from the frozen loaf and slotted them into the toaster.

'Sssh!' Her father held up his hand for silence for the weather report, even though no-one was talking. This was a morning ritual.

'… signs of a break to the drought.'

Everyone leaned closer to the radio, the better to hear if their luck was about to change.

'A storm warning is issued for the Guildford area.'

'Yes!' Laine's father beamed around the table as he switched off the radio. 'Might beat those hard-hearted bastards at the bank after all.'

'So we're not going to move?'

'Over my dead body.'

'Well, I'm going. I've left school now. I can't stay in this place forever.' Laine cracked eggs into the pan. The fat sizzled and spat. Her stomach gave a hungry growl.

'Why not? Your mum worked at the tanning factory in town before we got married. She wasn't too proud to earn her living where she could.'

'The factory's about to close. You know that, Dad.'

'They haven't said so.'

'They don't have to. They're just sacking people gradually. Soon there'll be no-one left.'

'You can find a job somewhere else, then.'

'Where? Face it, Dad, the whole town is dying.' Beneath his anger, Laine sensed her father's love and concern for her, and his fear that she would leave them.

'It's a hard life, I know. But we need you here, Laine. Your brothers and I couldn't manage without you, you know.'

It was an old argument, one Laine knew she couldn't win. Full of resentment, she began to serve breakfast.

'What would you do if you left this place?' queried Tom. 'You don't know anything, Laine!'

'I know enough to do better than you at school!'

'So?' Tom shrugged. 'You don't need brains to be a farmer.'

'I don't want to be a farmer.'

'What do you want to be, then?'

'When I grow up, I'm going to marry the best and fairest knight in all the land.' The girl squatted beside a cow, squirting milk into a pail as she threw out the challenge to her brother. Long brown hair and dark blue eyes. She wore a smock made out of coarse material, so long it touched her rough boots.

'You know Father will never let you go.' The boy sounded quite matter of fact. He didn't look at his sister, concentrating instead on filling his own pail with milk.

'It's not fair! You'll go to Camelot when you're old enough. Why can't I go too?' The cow shifted uncomfortably as the girl's grip tightened on its teats.

'Who will look after Father and Tirre and me if you go to court?'

The girl remained silent.

'Sir Gawaine says that the ladies at court are very beautiful. And they're all in love with Sir Lancelot,' her brother continued.

'Then he is the one I shall marry!'

'Don't be daft, Elaine!' The boy let out a loud crow of laughter. 'Why would Sir Lancelot even notice you among the ladies in their silken gowns and glittering jewels? Besides, I've heard that Sir Lancelot looks at no-one but the queen, and she is the fairest and most beautiful of all the ladies.'

'You seem to know a great deal of court gossip, little brother.' Elaine stopped tormenting the cow and rose to her feet, giving the stool a fierce kick as she did so.

'Not so little,' the boy defended himself as he picked up the pails of milk and walked towards the door of the byre. His eyes were alight with excitement as he continued. 'Father says I may leave home as soon as I am twelve. He says our uncle will take me into his household and train me to be a squire. I mean to do all in my power to be brave, to rescue damsels in distress and fight for King Arthur and so earn a knighthood. One day I shall be Sir Lavaine, second only to Sir Lancelot, and I shall marry the most beautiful woman in Camelot. Not you, Elaine. I wouldn't ever marry you, even if you weren't my sister.' He laughed again, the sound echoed by the scornful cawing of a raven. It circled over the girl's head. Elaine looked up, her face young and vulnerable under its pitiless stare.

'I will go,' she told the bird. 'I will go to Camelot.'

'When I grow up, I'm going to marry the best and fairest knight in all the land.'

Laine heard the words in her mind as clearly as if she'd spoken them herself. But she didn't want to marry a knight. There was something else she wanted to do.

'Now I've left school, I'd really like to be a model. Or a film star. I want to be rich and famous.' Laine smiled at Tom, trying to make a joke of it even as she spoke her secret aloud. Travelling to exotic places, meeting important people and doing wonderful things. If you were thin and beautiful, you could go anywhere and do anything you wanted.

'You've seen the babes in the movies.' Tom gave a scornful laugh. 'You've got the big hair and the big boobs, but you're big everywhere else as well. You'll never be rich and famous the way you look now.'

Laine's fingers tightened around the frypan. It took all her strength of will not to chuck it at her brother.

'Aren't we good enough for you, is that it?' her father challenged.

Laine looked at his tired, lined face, burnt and scarred from years of exposure to the sun. She felt torn between love and pity for his hard lonely life and her own desperate need to escape. Her father had chosen the path he wanted to follow; surely she should have a choice too?

'I want to go.' They were the hardest words she'd ever had to say. 'I could always come back and visit you.'

'You'll just pop over from London, or Paris, or New York?'

Laine caught a glimpse of herself in the squat metal teapot. She looked like a gargoyle, a blimp, her face and body distorted by the curves of its shining surface. She snatched up the frypan and, in despair, scooped the last of the eggs and sausages onto her father's plate.

'Not eating?' he queried.

'I'm not hungry.' She threw the empty pan into the sink and raced out of the house.

'When I'm fifteen, I shall go to Camelot. I'm going to marry the best and fairest knight in all the land,' Elaine told her father.

'You'll have to find someone who's deaf, dumb and blind, then.' Tirre roared with laughter at his own wit.

Elaine threw a piece of bread at him. 'Compose yourself, Elaine,' her father reproved his daughter. 'This is not seemly behaviour for a young girl.'

'There's only you and my brothers to see me,' Elaine sulked. 'No-one else ever comes near this place.'

Full of resentment, she looked out through the shutters to the forest beyond. Huge trees filtered the sunlight into thin rays of gold that slanted through the green dimness with an illusory brightness. The air was thick and damp. It seemed to Elaine that her life had been lived to the sound of rain dripping through the softly breathing trees, the cries of birds, the sharp bark of a fox. Once the forest's green softness had seemed sweet and inviting, but lately it had felt more like an impenetrable barrier that kept her from the outside world.

'We had a visitor only last week,' her father protested. 'Sir Gawaine brought us news of Camelot. We are well in touch with the outside world, child.'

'Sir Gawaine stayed only long enough to tell us he was lost and ask directions as to which path he should follow. You wouldn't allow me to listen to what little he had to say of Camelot, even though my brothers were granted an audience.'

'Gossip. Not fit for a girl's tender ears,' her father fussed.

'I'm fourteen years old, Father. Almost old enough to marry and have babies of my own. Surely I am old enough to listen to what the good knight had to tell us?' Elaine smiled at her father, her eyes full of hope. 'I did overhear him boasting of Sir Lancelot, how brave he is, how like a lion on the battlefield, how like a god to gaze upon. I wish to meet him, Father. Perhaps he is my destiny?'

'Your destiny lies here with us, Elaine.'

'But Tirre will go to court when he is old enough, and so will Lavaine. Why can't I go too?'

'Tirre must make his way in the world, and he will do so once he becomes a knight, but Lavaine is still only a child. You must stay here to help me rear him.'

'You promised I might go to Camelot once I turned fifteen.'

'I made the promise before your mother died, Elaine. You fill her place now. We need you here to look after us.'

'Father, I long to go to court. I long to see King Arthur and his queen, and meet Sir Lancelot. The fairest and bravest knight in all the world already holds a place in my heart.'

'Even if you had a pretty gown you could never compete for Sir Lancelot's favour.' Tirre gave a scornful snigger. 'The ladies at court are rich and very beautiful. They are skilled in music and poetry and other womanly arts which I'm sure do not include cooking meals and the lowly duties of a dairymaid! You should consider yourself lucky we don't mind taking you just as you are, Elaine.'

'Serve the meal, good daughter,' her father said gently. 'You must forget your dreams of Sir Lancelot. He is not for you, this much I have learned from Sir Gawaine. Your duty is here, with us. You will save yourself much sorrow and disappointment if you heed my warning and accept your fate.'

Biting back bitter words, Elaine set slices of bread onto the wooden trenchers in front of her brothers and father, then began to ladle out a stew made from hares trapped by Tirre, and herbs and vegetables from her garden.

Her father wrinkled his nose and sniffed suspiciously. 'What is this?' He took a cautious mouthful while Elaine continued to serve her brothers. 'It's not bad, I suppose.' He continued to eat, stuffing his mouth full and chewing noisily.

Elaine looked at the food in front of her. Her glance shifted to her waist. Surely she was losing her childhood plumpness? Her gown had felt looser of late. She pinched up some of the fabric, testing the space between fabric and belly. If the knights at court were handsome, then the ladies would be slim and beautiful. How could she, a baron's daughter reared in isolation in the forest, hope to compare with them? And yet the visiting knight had seemed courteous when her father had introduced them.

'This is my daughter, Elaine.'

Surely it had not been mere chivalry but real admiration in Sir Gawaine's eyes as he'd swept her a bow and said, 'The lady is as fair a lily as any I have seen at court.' Elaine pushed her trencher away so she wouldn't have to look at it, or smell her own delicious stew.

'Not eating?' Her father scooped some of her portion onto his own trencher and licked his lips.

'I have no appetite.' Elaine pushed back her seat and stood up. 'If you'll excuse me, Father?' Straight-backed she walked out, not waiting for his reply. But inwardly, she raged and wept, and cursed her fate.

She made for the river, for the watery highway leading to freedom, to Camelot. She stared down into the ripples, seeking reassurance, but her image appeared distorted and grotesque in the wrinkled surface of the water. A shadow passed over her, with a raucous caw that sounded like human laughter. Startled, Elaine looked upwards, straight into the cold, merciless eyes of the black raven. In that moment, she knew that she was lost. Blindly, desperately, she searched for the companion of her dreams, the companion who promised escape and freedom.

Freedom. She knew the word, yet the green barrier told her that freedom was an illusion. She must stay home and hide her ugliness. Her family had need of her and she would fulfil her duty to them, just as her dear mother would have wished.

Once outside, Laine kept on running, trying to outpace her thoughts. She was trapped here. Trapped by her father's need, by duty, and by her own fear. Her brothers were right. She was ugly. She'd never be able to make it in the real world. Tears coursed down her cheeks as she felt once again the black despair of her dream. Great wings of fear beat in her chest: the fear of escape, the fear of being trapped here forever. Sobbing and gasping for breath, she stopped at last and bent over, feeling the ache in her heart spread all through her body.

Above her, black clouds bellysurfed the sky, sending shadows scudding across the parched red earth beneath them. A few drops fell and, as Laine tilted her face to welcome them, thunder crashed and the sky split open in a blaze of light.

'When I grow up, I'm going to marry the best and fairest knight in all the land.'

Laine froze into stillness. 'You're the girl from my dream,' she whispered. 'Who are you? Why are you here?'

'When I grow up, I'm going to marry the best and fairest knight in all the land.'

Laine inspected the empty landscape. Nothing to see, yet she could feel the shadow's presence beside her, as real and close to her as a sister. She could sense also the girl's desperation to escape, her longing for freedom.

Marry a knight?

No, she thought. I don't have to marry to save myself. Nor do I have to live the life my father has chosen for me. Who I am and what I want is much more important than how I look. If I find out what I can do, what I want to do, I can choose my own path to freedom. She turned to the shadow, seeking reassurance, and felt a ghostly touch on her cheek, light and warm as a blessing.

The rain fell harder, stinging sheets of water that quickly churned the earth into a sea of red mud. Soaked to the bone, Laine took to her heels once more, running for the highest tree in the yard rather than her home.

The water would rise and the boat would come, she knew it would. When it did, she would be ready. And so would her shadow.

AUTHOR'S NOTE

My introduction to Arthurian legend came through reading 'The Lady of Shalott', the beautiful poem by Alfred Lord Tennyson. Questions haunted me: who was she? Why was she trapped in a tower and why was a curse put on her? Why did she have to die once she looked out of the window and saw Sir Lancelot? To answer these questions, which form the basis of the *Shalott* trilogy, I found myself reading and researching both the legend and the 'history' of King Arthur.

Mystery surrounds the real identity of the Lady of Shalott. Perhaps she was Elaine of Corbenic, daughter of King Pelles, who tricks Lancelot into lying with her after she assumes the likeness of Queen Guinevere.

From their union Galahad is born, the perfect knight who succeeds in achieving the Holy Grail. In some versions of the story, Lancelot and Elaine live together for a while, but Lancelot cannot keep away from Guinevere. He returns to court and Elaine dies.

It is more likely, however, that Tennyson took his inspiration from another Elaine, and it is this character I've used as a basis for this story and my novels. In Thomas Malory's *Le Morte d'Arthur*, Elaine of Astolat lives with her father and brothers in an area now identified as Guildford. The fate of the Fair Maiden of Astolat is to nurse Lancelot back to health after he is wounded in a forest nearby, and to fall in love with him. Lancelot wears Elaine's favour in the tourney for the Ninth Diamond, but he will neither marry her nor take her as his mistress. In despair, Elaine falls into a decline and dies. Her brother, Sir Lavaine, takes her body by boat to Camelot and delivers a letter from his sister to Lancelot in which she speaks of her love and asks Lancelot to bury her and pray for her soul.

In my story, I try to show that love and duty come at a price, as does fear. Although the two Elaines are separated by many centuries, their situations are similar. Perhaps their fates reflect the differing expectations and possibilities of their times, but it always takes courage — and a certain amount of selfishness — to break free and follow a dream.

ḣEARṪ'S ḊESIRE

Garth Nix

'To catch a star you must know its secret name and its place in the heavens,' whispered Merlin, his mouth so close to Nimue's ear his breath tickled and made her want to laugh. Only the seriousness of the occasion stopped a giggle. Finally, after years of apprenticeship, Merlin was about to tell her what she had always wanted to know, what she had worked towards for seven long years.

'You must send the name to the sky as a white bird. You must write it in fire upon a mirror. You must wrap the falling star with your heart's desire. All this must be done in the single moment between the end of night and the dawning of the day.'

'That's it?' breathed Nimue. 'The final secret?'

'Yes,' said Merlin slowly. 'The final secret. But remember the cost. Your heart's desire will be consumed by the star. Only from its ashes will power come.'

'But my heart's desire is to have the power!' exclaimed Nimue. 'How can I gain it and lose it at the same time?'

'Even a magus may not know their own heart,' said Merlin heavily. 'And it will be the whole desire of your heart, from past, present or future. You will be giving up something that may yet come to pass, if you choose not to take a star from the sky.'

Merlin looked at her as she stared up at the sky, watching the stars. He saw a young woman, with the dark face and hair of a Pict, her eyes flashing with excitement. She was not beautiful, or even pretty, but her face was strong and lively and every movement hinted at energy barely contained. She wore a plain white dress, sleeveless but stretching to her ankles, and bracelets of twisted gold wire and amethysts. Merlin had given her the bracelets, and they were invested with the many lesser magics that Nimue had learned from him in the last three years.

There were other things that Merlin saw, out of memory and with the gift he had taken from a falling star.

There was the past, beginning when a headstrong girl no more than fourteen years old sought him out in his simple house upon the Cornish headland. He had turned her away, but she had sat on his doorstep for weeks, living off shellfish and seaweed, until at last he had relented and taken her in. At first he had refused to teach her magic, but she had won that battle as well. He could not deny that she had the gift, and he could not deny that he enjoyed the teaching. Over the years that enjoyment in teaching her had become something else, though Merlin had never shown it. He was nearly three times her age, and he had spent many years before Nimue's arrival preparing himself for the sorrow that must come. He had not expected it to be as straightforward as simply falling in love with an impossible girl, but there it was.

There was the present, the two of them standing upon the black stone with the new sun shining down upon them.

The future, so many possible roads stretching out in all directions. If he wished, Merlin could try and steer Nimue towards one future. But he did not. The choice would be hers.

'My heart's desire is to gain full mastery of the Art,' Nimue said slowly. 'I can only gain that mastery by the capture of a star, yet that capture depends upon the sacrifice of my heart's desire. An interesting conundrum.'

'You should stay here and think on it,' said Merlin. He stepped down from the black stone, the centrepiece of the ring of stones that he had built almost twenty years before. The black stone had been the most difficult, though it was small and flat, unlike the standing monoliths of granite. He had drawn it out of the very depths of the earth, and it had smoked and run like water, before he forced it into its current shape. 'But breakfast calls me and I wish to answer.'

Nimue smiled and sat cross-legged on the stone. She watched Merlin as he walked away. As he left the ring of stones, the air shimmered around him, bright shafts of light weaving and dancing around his head and arms. The light sank into his hair and skin, and when it finally settled, Merlin's hair was white and he appeared to be much older than he really was. It was a magical disguise he had long assumed, Nimue knew. Age was associated with wisdom, and Merlin had also found it useful to appear aged and infirm. Nimue expected she would probably do the same when she came into her power. A crone was always much more convincing than a maiden.

Not that she expected to be a maiden too much longer. Nimue had her own plans for that step from maiden to woman grown. Merlin was part of that plan, though he did not know it. No village boy or even one of Arthur's warriors would do for Nimue. Merlin was the only man she had ever wanted in her bed. There had been some who had tried to influence her choice over the past few years, against all her discouragement. A few were still around, croaking and sunning their warty hides down in the reedy margins of the lake. Nimue was surprised they had lived so long. Most men died from such transformations. Sometimes she fed them flies, but she never let them touch her, either as toads or men.

Nimue turned her thoughts from failed suitors back to the conundrum presented by Merlin. Her heart's desire was to have the power, yet she would lose her heart's desire to gain the power. How could this be?

She scratched her head and lay down on the rock, letting the heat from the sun fall upon her. Unconsciously, she turned her palms up to catch the rays. The sun was a source of power, one she used in many lesser magics. It was good to take in the sun's power when the sky was clear, and she no longer needed to even think about it. Nimue could draw power from many sources: the sun, the earth, the moving stream, even the spent breath of animals and men.

What had Merlin lost, Nimue wondered. What was his heart's desire? He must have wanted the power as she wanted it. He had gained it, and as far as she could see he had lost nothing. He was the pre-eminent wizard of the age. The counsellor and maker of kings. There was no knowledge he did not have, no spell he did know.

Perhaps there was nothing to lose, Nimue thought.

Or if there was, it would be something she would never miss. A heart's desire that could come to pass, but did not, was no loss. To see the future was not the same as to live it. Perhaps she would see her heart's desire in the hearth fire, and would know it could never be. How much of a loss was that?

Nothing, thought Nimue. Nothing compared to the exhilaration of magic.

'Tonight,' she whispered and she curled up on the black stone like a cat resting up in preparation for extensive wickedness. 'Tonight, for everything.'

Merlin was not asleep when she came to his chamber. He lay on his bed, his eyes open, gleaming in the thin shaft of moonlight from the tower window. Nimue hesitated at the door, suddenly shy and afraid. She had chosen to come naked, but with her long dark hair artfully arranged to both cover and suggest. She had taken a long time to get her hair exactly right, and it was held in place with charms as well as pins.

'Merlin,' she whispered.

Merlin did not respond. Nimue drifted into the room. Her skin seemed to glow with an inner light and her smile promised many pleasures. Any man would rise and take her to his bed in eager haste. But not Merlin.

'Merlin. I shall go to the black rock before the dawn. But I would go as a woman, who has known her man. Your woman.'

'No,' whispered Merlin. He did not move, but lay as still as the chalk carving on the green of the hill. 'There are men a-plenty in the village. Two of Arthur's knights are visiting tonight. They are both good men, young and unmarried.'

Nimue shook her head and stepped forward. Her hair fell aside as she knelt by the bed, her magic dissolving and the pins unable to hold on their own.

'It is you I want,' she said fiercely. 'You! No one else. You want me too! I know it, as well as I know the ten thousand names of the beasts and the birds that you have taught me.'

'I do,' whispered Merlin. 'But I am your teacher, and it is not meet that we should lie together now, unequal in years and power. Go back to your own place.'

Nimue frowned. Then she rose and stamped her foot, and whirled away, light and shadows dancing in her wake. At the door, she looked back and her smile shone through the dark room.

'Tomorrow, I shall be my own mistress and you will not be master,' said Nimue. 'I will catch my star and we can be as man and wife.'

Merlin did not move or answer. In an instant, Nimue was gone, and the room was silent once more. The shaft of moonlight slowly crawled over Merlin's face, and darkness hid the tears that welled up out of his clear blue eyes. Young man's eyes, unclouded by age or glamour.

'Ah well,' he muttered to himself. 'Ah well.'

They were the words Merlin's father had said upon his deathbed. Simple words, devoid of magic, greeting a fate that could not be turned aside.

Nimue did not go back to her own bed. Instead she put on her best linen dress, that she herself had dyed blue from isatis bark and stitched with silver thread that she had spun out of the deep earth.

The silver thread shone in the moonlight as she slipped out of the house and out onto the headland. There was a pool at the edge of the western cliff, a pool of soft water, fed by spring and rain. It was always placid, mirror-like, in sharp contrast to the sea that crashed on the rocks only a few paces away, but two hundred feet below. An ancient hawthorn tree leaned over the pool, all shadows and spiky branches. It had often been mistaken in the dark for a giant, or some fell creature. Every midwinter night, some hapless stranger would seek to use the power of the pool, only to flee in panic from the hawthorn. Invariably they found the cliff edge and the pounding sea that would grind their bones to dust.

Nimue stood at the edge of the pool and hugged herself against the bite of the wind, cold in this early morning. She whispered to herself, preparing for what must be done:

'To find the secret name of a star
Ask the moon that shares the sky
Fix its place between the branches of the hawthorn tree
Send the name to the sky on the wings of a bird
Burn the name in fire upon the mirrored waters of the lake
Wrap the star with heart's desire
Between the darkness and the light
Then you shall a magus be ...'

Nimue looked up to the heavens and found the great disc of the moon, yellow as ancient cheese. She let its light fall upon her face and open hands, and took in its power. But a yellow moon was not what she sought. She waited, silent, the hawthorn tree softly groaning in the wind, the surf crashing deep below.

Slowly the moon began to sink and change. The yellow faded and blue-silver began to spill across its face. Nimue felt the change and smiled. Soon she would ask it to name her star. She had already chosen one. A bright star, but not so bright it might overpower her. Not the Evening Star, that served no-one and never would. But a star as bright as Merlin's, though not as red. She would be his equal in power, if not in kind.

A bird called, the sleepy cry of something woken before its time. The wind fell and the hawthorn stilled. Nimue felt a tremor rush through her. Dawn was only minutes away. The moon was silver, she must act.

She called to the moon, a call that no human ears

could hear. At first there was no answer, but she had expected that. She called again, using the power she'd drawn earlier from the sun. The moon grew a fraction brighter at the call, and through the void, her silver voice came down, quiet and imbued with sadness, speaking for Nimue alone.

'Jahaliel.'

As the name formed in her head, Nimue sank to one knee and looked up through the branches of the hawthorn. There, in the fork where two twisted branches met, she saw her star, bright between two strands of darkness.

Nimue splashed her hand in the pool and the droplets flew into the air to become a white bird, a dove whose wings made a drum-roll as it rose straight up towards the sky, the name of the star held in its beak where once it would have carried an olive branch.

The pool was still before Nimue's hand had left it, still and shining, reflecting the woman, the tree, the moon and sky. With her forefinger and all that was left of the sun's power within her, Nimue wrote in fire upon the mirrored water, the three runes that spelled out the name 'Ja-hal-iel'.

In the heavens, a star fell. The moon sank, and the sun rose.

In the instant between night and day, Nimue caught her star and bound it forever with the promise of her heart's desire.

She felt something leave her, and tears started in her eyes. But she did not know what she had lost, and the exultation of power was upon her.

Nimue ran to the cliff top and threw herself into the air. Like a feather she drifted down, buffeted this way and that by the wind, but taking no harm. Before the cold water embraced her, she became a dolphin, plunging into a wave, sliding under the water to spin out the other side, laughing as only a dolphin can.

Nimue had been a dolphin before, but it was Merlin who had made her so. It was his star's power that had given her the shapes of many things, on sea and air and land. Now she could transform herself at will. She jumped again and between two waves became a hawk, shooting up above the spray. A merlin, to be exact, and that was her joke and tribute. On bent-back wings she sped across the headland, past the pool, towards the rising sun and Merlin.

With sharp hawk eyes she saw he had already risen, and was waiting for her in the ring of stones. He stood upon the black rock, without a glamour upon him, and Nimue felt love from him rise in her heart as bright and strong as the rising sun.

She flew still higher, until she was directly above him and he had to shade his eyes to look at her. Then she folded her wings and dropped straight down, down into his open arms.

They had one kiss, one brief embrace, before the

stars they wore pushed them apart, the air itself wrenching them from each other's grasp. Nimue shouted and directed her will upon her new-found power, but to no avail. She was pushed completely off the black stone, to fall sprawling in the circle.

Merlin did not shout. He had fallen on his back, and was sinking into the black stone, as if it were not stone at all, but some peaty bog that had trapped an unwary traveller.

He did not shout, but his voice was loud and clear in Nimue's ear as she struggled to her feet.

'You were my heart's desire, Nimue, waiting in the future. You were the price I paid for the art. Love never to be fulfilled. Forgive me.'

His hand stretched up from the stone. Nimue snatched at it, as if even now she might somehow pull him back. But her hand closed on empty air, and his disappeared beneath the surface of the stone.

'Forgive me, Merlin,' whispered Nimue. She made no effort to stem the tears that fell upon the stone. A bright star shone in the hollow of her neck, the promise of power and wisdom beyond anything she had ever dreamed. But she was cold inside, cold with the knowledge that this power was not her heart's desire. Her true heart's desire lay entombed in dark stone, beyond her reach forever.

Or was he? Nimue clutched her star and looked up at the sky, so bright above her. If a star could be plucked from the sky, then surely it could also be made to rise again? To take its place in the firmament once more, unravelling all the threads of time that had been woven in its fall. If she could return her star, then surely Merlin would freely walk the earth, and he in turn could free his star and regain his heart's desire.

There were other powers in the world. Other places to find knowledge. Nimue stretched her slim arms above her head and in a moment was a bird, wide-winged and far-sailing. She rode a wind west, across the open sea, and was gone from Britain.

With her went all Merlin's wisdom and power, and all hope for the kingdom of Arthur. The kingdom that would sink into ruin as Nimue's heart's desire had sunk into the stone.

AUTHOR'S NOTE

I have always been interested in the relationship between Merlin and Nimue, who is also sometimes known as Vivian. There are many variations of their story, but traditionally it goes something like this:

'The witch Nimue sought Merlin's power and wormed her way into his confidence. He became infatuated with her and taught her much of his magic. Finally, while demonstrating to her how someone could be magically imprisoned in a cave, Merlin was trapped himself and Nimue inherited most of his magical power. With Merlin entombed forever, King Arthur lost his most important adviser and magician. As Nimue wasn't interested in taking Merlin's role, this was where everything started to go wrong for Arthur.'

I'm not the first author to wonder why Merlin, the most powerful sorcerer of the age and a seer who could see the future, would let himself be entrapped. Of course, otherwise wise and powerful people often do make terrible errors of judgment when lust or love is involved. But they can't see the future and Merlin could. I'm sure if Bill Clinton could have seen his own future we would never have heard of Monica Lewinsky.

If Merlin could see what was going to happen, why did he teach Nimue, why did he let himself be entombed? There had to be a reason.

One of my favourite Arthurian-related fantasies is *Merlin's Mistake* by Robert Newman. In that book, Merlin simply got sick of Nimue always going on at him and let himself be locked away to get some peace and quiet. In a short play I've written called 'The Compleat Arthur', Merlin suggests it was a property settlement after their divorce: he got the house and Nimue got the power.

In 'Heart's Desire' I have looked for a more serious explanation of the true nature of a relationship between a man and a woman whose lives were complicated by power, magic and destiny. I also wanted to explore the character of Nimue, to find someone who was more than just a power-hungry witch.

ᚈhe ᚹork of ᚷiants

Lucy Sussex

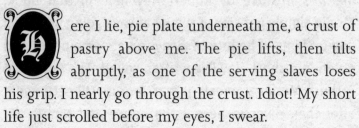

ere I lie, pie plate underneath me, a crust of pastry above me. The pie lifts, then tilts abruptly, as one of the serving slaves loses his grip. I nearly go through the crust. Idiot! My short life just scrolled before my eyes, I swear.

There's a lot of swearing going on outside the pie too, until Raven takes command: 'Shut up! I said, *shut up!*'

Sudden obedient silence.

'All lift together. Ready? One, two, three!'

The pie rises again, then settles onto the serving slaves' shoulders.

'Now, march!'

The pie lurches forwards, swaying like Raven's boat on the sea. It makes me queasy and I send up a prayer to whoever is my god (or patron saint, as the Christians say) not to be sick. That's all I need, to meet my new boss with my armour all covered in vomit.

There are fifty steps between the kitchen and the warlord Claudius's banqueting hall, adult steps, not mine. Raven and I, we checked out the route yesterday. I rode on his back like a hunch, muffled in his cloak against the sea wind, and also curious eyes. Claudius wants his present for the king to be a surprise, just as Raven wants to be prepared. Good villains prepare down to the smallest detail, that's Raven's rule. Sure, Raven, but if this works I'm not a villain anymore. Me and my big sisters, older and younger, we'll be fixed for life, protected and fed. If these clumsy oafs don't drop and kill me first.

That's how all my troubles started, when the midwife went and dropped me on my head. Or so I'm told, though everyone who knew me then is dead: from sickness, starving, stolen for slaves or killed by raiders — the usual stuff. It'd make me weep if I wasn't flat-out keeping what's left of my family alive. We look after ourselves, me and my two sisters, scavenging and stealing, scraping a scapegrace living out of what used to be Roman Britannica. Which is now mostly Roman remains, what the legions left behind when they went marching home and things all fell to bits.

Just like a handworked pottery pie-plate would, if it was dropped from shoulder height. I try not to remember that the serving slaves were ill-matched in height (though not as much as Raven and me), and one was lame. All the worse to carry me with. Not to mention the route itself! Claudius's hill-fort isn't Roman work, but older, made of rough-hewn stone, or stone not hewn at all. That means fifty places where a foot might strike an uneven bit of paving and trip, dropping the king-sized pie.

The pie wobbles as the kitchen door is negotiated. Again, I see my life, a Roman scroll going past at speed. The faces of my sisters, Marcella and Petra living, the others dead. All the people we begged from, or robbed. Sorry, but we were just trying to survive. That's why I invented the somersault dance, for when times were sort of good, and people would give stray kids a feed for making them laugh. And that's why I invented the basket heist, also known as the package heist, or the bundle of firewood heist. For the winter months, or any time when things were hard and nobody gave anything away. Remind me never to do that again, especially not near the coast.

We're in the courtyard now. Plenty of rough flagstones here, all the better to smash me dead in a shroud of pastry and razor-sharp pottery shards. Hey, you idiots, Marcella might only be twelve, but she carries me better than you do! Except for that last time, when she dropped me and I landed in this mess. Marcella, if wishes were horses, I'd go back in my life and change it, so that I don't end up in a sarcophagus of pie plate with a crusty lid.

Back to the day we met Raven, that's a good place. Back to a little hilltop woodlet, a moon or so back.

'I wish we had a pot to carry you in, Nimus,' my younger sister Petra had said. 'One of those old amphorae from the burnt-out villa. You'd just fit.'

Marcella frowned. 'Too heavy.'

'Don't see why. Nimus ain't growed since last time, and we've never used a pot before.'

'Yes, but you don't have to carry him … Unless you really want to, amphora and all.'

Petra looked down at me. 'I'm too small!'

'Stop squabbling,' I said. 'Twigs it is. Now go and collect a bundle of them.'

When we had enough twigs, they tied them densely around me so I was completely covered, invisible to the watchful eye. Then Marcella hefted me onto her back and we took the old overgrown Roman road down to the coast, and a farming settlement. It was the typical sort of place, fortified walls and ditch, with a watchtower for raiders on a nearby hill. They held a market day every few moons, two fowls traded for a bag of grain, eggs for loaves, if we were lucky, trade goods from over the seas. If we were really unlucky, we'd end up being traded ourselves. That was the danger of getting too close to the sea these days.

My legs I tucked up inside the bundle, a shorter bunch of twigs hiding my head. From the peephole I could see Petra skipping along the road in front of us in tunic and leggings. A good disguise — one happy little boy, followed by an older lad being responsible, carrying a bundle of wood to sell. Nothing to show we meant villainy.

After a couple of hours we neared the fort, which was surrounded by a double defensive ditch. Its drawbridge was down and the market spread across the clearing in front of it.

'Guards?' I murmured into Marcella's ragbag cape.

'Mostly on the drawbridge.' She drew in her breath sharply. 'They're searching everybody going into the settlement.'

'Had trouble here before, then. All right, let's stay outside for the moment, check out the marketplace.'

I peered through the peephole, saw the usual homespun clothing, then the flash of sun on grey metal — weapons. Next moment the ass-end of a donkey, no a mule, a big one, carrying panniers. Covet covet covet. Then a gleam of gold brooch, necklace, earrings. Must be the settlement boss, no it's his missus. Ah, missuses, plural. Covet their gold a lot more, but it's out of our league.

'Where's Petra?' I murmured.

'Scouting. Trying to get over the drawbridge.'

The usual procedure with the basket heist is that my sisters arrive at a likely fortification with a bundle. They deposit it somewhere quiet inside, leave the fort and wait nearby for night. People don't usually get suspicious of the bundle, it's so small, couldn't possibly be anyone inside. When all I can hear is snoring, I get out of the bundle, case the joint on tiptoe, find something worth stealing. If it's more than I can carry, I let the others in to help. Then we make ourselves scarce with the stolen goods. We don't take much, we aren't greedy, just enough to survive. A sack of dried beans, or some grain — that'd be nice, last us to harvest time.

I wished, I coveted, but I was getting a bad feeling about this place. The people looked edgy and unhappy. Also, some here were up to no good. The man idly strolling by the stack of sheepskins, for example. He was middle-sized, middle-aged, nothing that stuck in the mind about him. A very useful way to look if you happen to be a villain, and he was circling around like a bird of prey. That said scavenger to me — it takes one to know one. He too was checking out this place.

Petra returned, innocently taking Marcella's hand, leaning close.

'The guards have a cask of homebrew.'

'And are guzzling it?'

'Uh-huh.'

'Ah. Change of plan. Sooner or later a fight'll break out. When it happens we do a snatch and grab. Then scarper.'

We did another circuit of the market, choosing what to snatch. Petra eyed the mule, and I estimated the odds of getting away with it in one piece. We were still making up our group mind, when the trouble started, and not what we were expecting. From the direction of the watchtower someone tolled a bell.

'Scoti raiders again,' someone screamed. 'Men, to arms!'

Petra made a beeline for the mule, but somebody else got there first. That left only shanks ponies for us, in the middle of a panicking crowd. The guards at the drawbridge were drunkenly playing gatekeepers, picking who could go in, who stayed out. I saw an old countrywoman from the market knocked back by a blow from the blunt end of a spear. Those not trying for the fort were running across the flat, heading for the hills. We followed — if they had a hiding place, we wanted to know where it was.

Marcella had Petra by the hand, me on her back, as she scurried over the flat and up the nearest hill. It was low, but studded with large rocks, between them running a narrow pathway. As we toiled upwards I got jolted up and down, and just as we neared the crest, Marcella stumbled and lost her grip. I went rolling downwards, twigs and all. They turned out to be useful, forming a padding against the ground and the rocks, which otherwise might have mashed me. But I still had a dizzying, jolting, painful and scary trip down to the bottom of the hill. Finally a large tussock stopped my roll. I rocked upright and uncoiled my legs. All I could do was run up the hill to Petra again, fast as I could go, which wasn't very fast.

A shout sounded behind me, from the fort, its drawbridge up now: 'Sorcery!'

Well, I guess a bundle of sticks suddenly growing little legs might look like sorcery, if you were the superstitious kind. A spear whacked into the earth beside me. Not only superstitious, but a good shot! I pulled at the willow strap holding the twigs around my waist, trying to get rid of the bundle before it got me killed.

'Don't!' I heard another man yell. 'It's only a kid, little more than a baby.'

I threw the last twigs away and bolted for the path, not fast enough to miss the rejoinder: 'Funny-looking kid, though. Runt of the litter.'

Thump-ker-thump, thump-ker-thump came hoofbeats behind me, a horse running at speed. The raiders couldn't have got here so quickly, so it had to be someone local. I sneaked a glance over my shoulder, saw a horse face with ears long as dock leaves. The mule, and on its back the scavenging man from the market! As they neared, I turned and yelled, 'Give a kid a lift before the raiders get me?'

He blinked at the sight of me, and his mouth opened, like a hunting bird swooping for the kill. As the mule overtook he bent and scooped me up with one arm. Safety! Then he thrust me head downwards into the mule's pannier, which was damp from what smelt like homebrew. Now I was upside down, being jolted this way and that in my straw prison, as the mule followed the sheeptrack up the hill. I twisted and turned, trying to wriggle out, but a big hand held the pannier shut. The mule crested the hill, and reached the other side, away from the settlement. Then all of a sudden it shied, brayed earsplittingly, then stopped with a jerk.

I peered through the basket slats in the pannier. Petra and Marcella stood on rocks either side of the path, each grasping a long hairy mule ear with one hand. With the others they held Marcella's cape over the animal's head, blinding it. The mule shook its huge head, but couldn't dislodge them.

'Let go of the mule!'

'No. Let go of my brother!' said Marcella.

'You and whose army, boy?'

He'd drawn a knife, I could see its gleam in the afternoon light.

I twisted in the pannier, but he still held it closed. 'You idiots! Go away, run, don't mind me,' I shouted.

'We stick together, we go where he goes.' That was Petra.

'Not into slavery,' I yelled. 'Go on, vamoosh!'

The man kicked the pannier. 'Shut up, you!'

'Marcella, grab her, run!' I screamed. Then I punched myself, realising the mistake.

'You two are girls?' the man said. I could guess where his thoughts were going, and didn't like it one bit.

'Yes, and worth more than Nimus. I'm almost grown up, Petra only wants a few years. So let him go, take us instead.'

The man said, 'Two able-bodied girls for this Nimus in the basket? That's not much of a deal.'

He's mad, I thought. Or greedy. 'Go on, run,' I yelled. 'Before the Scoti get us all!'

The man laughed. 'Scoti, what Scoti?'

'The alarm …'

'My sidekick.'

I thought about it a moment, smelling the homebrew in the pannier. 'Get the guards drunk,' I said. 'Create a diversion, snatch and grab, then scarper with mule and anything small and valuable. I'd guess the gold jewellery the boss's women were flaunting.'

When the man spoke again, he sounded like he'd been thinking too.

'Guessed right. And I'd guess that Nimus didn't disguise himself as firewood for any honest reason, and you two handy girls with an ambush are his sidekicks.'

Marcella nodded wearily.

'Then we're fellow travellers. We can talk business.'

Huh?

'But not right now. The settlement boss'll realise he's been burned, and I mean to be far away when he does. Unhand the mule and follow me.'

'Put the knife away first,' I said.

He sheathed it at his belt.

'You're not gonna sell my brother into slavery?' said Petra.

He pulled me out of the pannier and set me on the saddlebow before him. 'Not without his permission. Now let's scram!'

And that was how we met Raven. He led the way up the coast, me riding, and the girls trotting alongside. Towards dusk we came to a little cove, with a rowboat waiting on the sand. I guessed the rower was the sidekick who'd set off the diversionary alarm in the watchtower. Raven lifted me off the mule and gave it a lick of salt for services rendered. Then it got a smack on the rump to send it galloping off.

We piled into the boat and rowed out into the bay. Around the headland was a larger boat, trader size.

'You steal that too?' I said.

He eyed me. 'Sometimes I steal, sometimes I trade. I'm a dealer, a do-it man. People want something, I get it, even if I have to sail to Gaul or Ireland.'

When we reached the boat, a rope ladder came down for us. Up on the deck, I swayed in the sea motion and grabbed the mast for support.

The crewman coiling the ladder glanced around, and his pale eyes went wide.

He pointed at me and babbled in some unknown tongue. I only caught the word 'kobold'.

Raven answered in the same language. 'Guthlaf thinks you're supernatural,' he said.

'Yes, people do sometimes.' I stepped towards Guthlaf, so that I was almost level with his trembling knees. Whatever he thought I was, it scared him a lot. Good.

'I can't translate exactly,' said Raven. 'I'm not good at Guthlaf's lingo yet. But I'd say he thinks you're like what in Ireland they call the little folk. How old are you?'

'Eleven.'

'And tall as a two-year-old.'

The sidekick rummaged in a deck locker and pulled out a knotted measure string. He threw it to Raven, who caught it and measured me, top to toe. His scavenger eyes appraised me.

'Amazing,' he said.

'That's our Nimus,' Petra said fondly.

'Minimus really,' added Marcella. 'The smallest one.'

Raven stood up. 'Guthlaf here, he's a barbarian. He sees a ruined Roman basilica, he calls it "enta geworc".'

'Enta geweorc,' said Guthlaf, correcting the pro-nunciation despite his fear .

'The work of giants.'

From down here, I thought, you're all giants to me.

'Guthlaf doesn't believe anything that big was built by humans. He's never seen Rome, he's never heard that cultured, important people collect Nimuses. They like having little people around to amuse them, take their mind off affairs of state. Ever hear of one Lucius? He was court dwarf to the Emperor Augustus. Led a cushy life he did, three meals a day, fine clothes.'

'Nice work for those who can get it,' I said.

'There aren't many dwarves around. Which means, rarity value. I've got a client on the south coast, name of Claudius. He was Claw when he was just a plain old robber, but now he's a warlord. He apes the purple, puts on all sorts of Roman airs and graces. But he's small fry compared with that new king in the west.'

'Ambrosius Aurealianus?' said Marcella.

'You've heard of him?'

'He beat off the Sassenach raiders!' butted in Petra.

'He's something else, Claudius reckons. A Britannic Caesar in the making, who'll beat off the Sassenachs and the Scoti forever. That's why Claudius is making an alliance with him. And he wants a present, something that'll really impress the king. He asked me to import a lion. As if! I was looking for something to fob him off with, and I find young Nimus here.'

'You're going to sell Nimus into slavery!' wailed Petra.

'I'm going to get him a job, for life. You know how to dance, do cute tricks?'

I nodded. Swaying on the decking, feeling my first ever seasickness, there and then I did the somersault dance. It had been a tough day, I was not at my best, but still I made Raven and his crew laugh.

'Not bad,' he said. 'But it needs a little tweaking. A costume, for certain. And it would help if your sisters could provide a musical accompaniment. Drums, at least.'

Over the next few days, as we sailed along the coast, Raven refined the dance, came up with a game plan. Which had to be discarded when we met Claudius, because he had his own ideas. Claudius had heard of a banquet for some Caesar, where dwarves jumped out of a great pie and staged a mock battle. He only had one dwarf, but he got his artisans making fake armour out of wood and leather, and bullied his cook into baking the biggest pastrycrust of his career. Which is how I became a fancy pie-filling, being carried like a dignitary on a litter into the banqueting hall.

Now I can hear the humming talk of the soldiers and courtiers as the slaves set down the plate on the high table. Somewhere near are Petra and Marcella, with two new hand-drums, ready to play. I draw my legs up, just as I had inside the bundle of twigs, away from the end where the knife is going. That's the signal for me to leap out and do the somersault dance for my new master.

He'd better like me, or else!

AUTHOR'S NOTE

Arthur and his court have generated so much fiction that there seems little imaginative space for a twenty-first-century author. Hence my decision to write about a character not named in the literature, and only mentioned in passing: Arthur's dwarf. In Malory's *Morte D'Arthur* dwarves have frequent walk-on parts. In his 'Sir Gareth of Orkney' a dwarf is kidnapped by a knight on horseback: he is later seen riding pillion behind the knight and described as a 'a lytel dwerf ... with heuy chere' (a little dwarf looking unhappy). The words stuck in my mind.

Court dwarves were a fixture of Roman and medieval courts, their role being somewhere between that of jester and pet. The tensions of this role are described in Nick Page's *Lord Minimus*, the life of Jeffrey Hudson, eighteen inches tall, and an English court dwarf from the age of seven. He was a Captain of Horse in the English civil war of the 1640s, fought a duel with pistols on horseback, and killed his opponent. From *Lord Minimus* I took my character's name and the detail of being served up in a pie to his royal boss, Queen Henrietta Maria. From an Iranian film, *A Time for*

Drunken Horses, I took the detail of a family of orphaned children, one of whom is a dwarf, struggling to survive. I also took the mule, but avoided getting him drunk.

the customs
of the country

Dave Luckett

he woods were open, and no barrier to horsemen who could pick their way. The column halted at the edge of the trees. Galadus made the gesture that means 'form line', and the others spread out on both sides. He walked his horse forward another ten paces or so, to overlook the last line of scrub. Before him lay open fields — good plough-land and meadow for as many as twenty horses. Real horses, not British ponies.

Galadus sniffed, and smelled smoke. The Pictii, having looted the village, were burning it. Soon they would be here to loot and burn the manor house as well. There it stood, three hundred paces away down a gentle slope. Once, it had been a hollow square around a formal garden. Lately, though, the square's outer faces had been fortified with cut stone obtained by dismantling the old inner rooms. A new timber and thatch hall hulked in the middle of the square, looking uncouth, but the morning sun glowed on a graceful stone colonnade across the front of the old building. Peleus had insisted on keeping that colonnade. A gentleman's residence, said he, should have something of an air to it.

Now the village's women and children had been gathered within its walls, and the men stood ready to defend them. Too few men. There were perhaps a hundred villagers, of which no more than forty were fighters. The raiders were five to one.

Galadus shifted in his saddle. Grandfather wouldn't like this. He'd had to work around Peleus before, though.

Peleus, as magistrate, heard Beren's opening statement, then cut it short. He leaned forward, wincing. 'The records are clear. Your late father cannot will this land to you, for he never owned it. It cannot be part of his estate. If you wish to *lease* it as Villanus did, no doubt Marcus Hortensius, the owner, will negotiate reasonable terms.' Peleus glanced at the cracked parchment on the table. 'Or his heirs will.'

Berenus — known anywhere else as Beren, son of Wielan — exchanged glances with his wife and daughter in the body of the hall, then looked up again at Peleus.

'Wielan, my father, had the land right —' Peleus's brows drew down, and Galadus, at the table, grimaced at the farmer. Beren took a deep breath. 'I beg the court's pardon. *Villanus*, my father, had the land right, and I am his son. This Marcus Hortensius is a foreigner, a Gaul, it is said.'

The magisterial brows only drew down further. Peleus gestured towards the document. 'It is recorded that he resides at Soissons, in Gaul, and he owns the land, or his heir does. There is no such thing as this land right you speak of. It's a barbarian notion, that a man can have rights to land just by farming it.'

The farmer spluttered, turning red in the face. Galadus cleared his throat and spoke. 'There is, so please the court, the matter of the land taxes.' The voice was expressionless, as became the clerk of a magisterial court, and mature beyond its owner's years. Galadus would be fifteen in the summer.

Peleus shifted in his seat. It was the backless chair of the Roman judge, and he could only straighten his spine with painful effort. 'What is the tax debt?' he asked coldly.

'Seven sesterces, Magister,' replied Galadus.

Beren started to say something, and his tone might have been angry, but the boy's hand and face twitched in negation and the farmer cut himself off, looking baffled.

The magistrate considered. 'Has the owner been told of it?' he asked.

Galadus stirred papers on the table. 'Yes, Magister. The court wrote to him two years ago, but he has made no reply. I have a copy of the letter here.'

'Mmm. Is there a prospective tenant willing to pay the outstanding taxes?'

Galadus nodded, and Beren recognised his cue. 'I, Beren son of ... I mean, Berenus son of Villanus, am willing to pay the heriot ... the land tax, that is. In kind. I offer a plough-ox.'

Peleus did not quite scowl, though his lips thinned. 'Judgment. The court confiscates such portion of the land as will represent the tax arrears, and in the absence of the owner, directs that the whole be leased to Berenus, on the same terms as his father. The clerk will collect both tax and rent.'

Galadus made a notation. 'So recorded,' he intoned. And then, 'Magister, that is the last case.'

'Court stands adjourned, then, until the Ides of Julius.' Peleus levered himself erect, turned, and paced slowly through the door behind him. He refused to hobble; his staff appeared to be carried only as a badge of office.

Galadus began gathering up his records. The farmer straightened from his bow, blew out a breath, and turned to receive the congratulations of his wife. Hilde, his daughter, left her mother's side and approached the table.

'Thanks for that,' she said, tucking a long dark curl into her coif. Hilde had inherited her mother's Celtic hair and her father's Saxon blue eyes, a combination that had strange effects on Galadus.

The boy shrugged his broad shoulders. 'It's nothing.'

'Not nothing. We'd have lost the land without you.'

Galadus shook his head. 'No. Grandfather is a reasonable man. He knows perfectly well who should hold it. We just had to give him a way of saying so.'

'But when he came out with that stupid idea that some Gaul in ... where was it?'

'Soissons.'

She showed white teeth. 'An odd name. Sounds like what you make from pig's innards.'

'It was overrun by the Alemanni thirty years ago. I don't suppose it sounds, or looks, much like anything now.'

'Well, thanks anyway. If you hadn't sent that writing I think your grandfather would have insisted on finding the fellow, and the legitimate land-right is Father's, as everybody knows.'

'But only God would know where the owner is now. Or his heir, if he had one, legitimate or no.'

Galadus spoke without expression. Beren was moving towards him. He addressed the farmer, and his voice became formal. 'You'll give the ox, then, and will have land right of your father's holding for your lifetime, on condition that you work on the tax land for one day in the week.'

Beren nodded, unsmiling. 'Done,' he said. He did not offer his hand, but this was, as both of them knew, the true bargain. 'Come along, Hilde. It's still a working day.'

She smiled and Galadus smiled back. She waved at him, a little flutter of her fingers, before she followed her parents out into the spring breeze.

He could see smoke on the breeze, now. The others stirred and muttered. Their homes were burning. He spoke, easily, naturally, just as if he were not sweating-sick himself.

'Wait, lads. They'll be here soon enough. We want them looking the other way when we hit them, and we want a nice clear space to work up to full pace. It's no place for horses, in among the houses.'

They subsided, grumbling. These were boys and youths. Any man with experience, Saxon or Briton, knew that warriors fought afoot. Well, all but one man with experience. Galadus looked back at Syragus, the stablemaster, and the leathery little man smiled.

Grandfather had accepted Galadus learning to ride. What Peleus didn't know was that Syragus taught the village boys, too. But Grandfather was not always so easily got around.

Peleus glared. 'Don't you understand? Until we civilise them, these people know nothing higher than their own kin. No state. No Empire. No government. Their bloodlines are everything to them. But if we accept their customs, as we did with Beren, we uphold barbarian tradition over written law. We fail to civilise them — and we weaken your own right to inherit.'

Galadus nodded stiffly, once. 'I understand, sir.'

'I wonder if you do. I adopted you and made you my heir. That's perfectly valid, in law. But these people know nothing of written law. They can't read. They've never heard of adoption.' He leaned forward, careless of the pain. 'If we follow their custom, you're a bastard. And bastardry would deny you your right, in their eyes. Do you really want what *they* think is right? They won't thank you for it, you know.'

Galadus said nothing. He knew it, and knew also that the alternative was a law that gave land to a man long-dead in a province long-lost. He could only bow his head again, jerkily, like a poorly-made puppet.

The old man sighed. 'Very well, I did wrong. But your father would not marry, because he wanted another, and my daughter would have only him. What was going to happen would have happened anyway. I thought to assure myself of an heir this way. But it will all go for nothing if the people will not recognise your adoptive right. Please consider that, Galadus, before you write any more letters that we both know can't be sent, on behalf of your village friends.'

Village friends. Galadus glanced at them, ranged to right and left behind him. Well, if this was going to work, it would be up to them. Up to him. Syragus was a foreigner and a servant. Galadus was at least free-born, the best rider and the biggest and strongest, a suitable war-leader. This was not a matter affecting their own inheritances, so they would follow him. Within reason.

He turned to his front again and drew a sharp breath. The path from the house to the village was broad, and the Pictii had appeared on it.

They could be called a crowd, for they made no attempt to march in ranks. But it was a crowd of armed men, and they kept together, a compact grey-brown mass, spreading out when they saw the house. Scattered glimmers reflected from spearhead or axe-blade. Here and there flecks of colour showed, where the wealthy boasted coloured cloaks or painted shields. Few had even a helmet. None had body-armour. But there were two hundred of them, and Galadus had fifteen riders, counting himself.

So he could only watch while they brought up a ram and some ladders. Then they spread out into their customary formation, a cloud of warriors around the chieftain in the centre. Another knot, probably the strongest men, formed around the ram.

Galadus waited. The youths were restless, looking towards him, anxious to be off. But this would not do. So many infantry would close around a mounted charge, enveloping the riders and dragging them down. The foot must be packed together, less able to move, and they must be taken by surprise. He must hit them in the rear while they were engaged to their front.

Brech was pushing his horse forward. Galadus stared at him and jerked his head at the line. Brech returned glare for glare, looking mutinous. Others muttered. He could not hold them much longer.

Then came Syragus's voice: 'It's as you say, master. They're moving now.'

Galadus swung around, Brech and his mutiny forgotten. It was true, though the barbarians could not all start together. Their front ranks had broken into a run before the rear began to move, but the crowd oozed down the slope towards the nearest wall of the house, yelling as they ran.

Galadus heard it, three hundred paces away. 'Yes. They'll all be looking that way, now. Walk. Remember, nobody rides ahead of me. We have to get there all together, with our horses still fresh.'

Custom was on his side. He'd been accepted as their war leader. By their customs, then, they'd obey him, but it was not the obedience of disciplined soldiers. So long as he led, they would follow. But he must lead them into battle. If they thought he was hanging back, they'd turn against him.

He walked his horse forward. The Pictii had reached the house, piling up at the base of the colonnade. Now there was a flicker of metal from the top of the wall, and arching sparks. They were throwing lit brands over the wall, to fire the structures within. The ram had begun to thud against the gates. Galadus kept to a walk, his eyes on them. They had to be jammed up more than this.

Smoke was rising. The gates were beginning to sag. There was just time.

And then a column collapsed. The barbarians had been rocking it, and it had suddenly broken into its component drums, dropping the lintel on them, which had apparently crushed several men. But the lintel was also part of the wall, and with its fall a piece of the wall collapsed as well. There was a sudden breach. The barbarians howled in rage and delight, and surged forward. They'd be in among the villagers in moments. They were crowding around the breach, all eager to be in at the sack. Galadus shook his spear high. He set his spurs.

It seemed to take only moments to reach a gallop, but Galadus knew it was longer. He remembered Syragus saying, in his odd accent: 'Harse is not hare, Galahad. Gif him hunhred pazes to rich a gallop.'

The light seemed to flare, and the ground became a green blur. His spear had levelled itself, without thought from him. All his thought, all his mind, was concentrated on that howling mob at the base of the ruined column. Behind him, a solid line of armoured riders lowered their lances into the charge.

Perhaps a few of the raiders heard, or felt the ground shudder. Faces had begun to show, as men turned their heads to look over their shoulders. But there was no time for them to react, no time but for a moment's gaping. Then the charge hit.

The spearhead and half the length of the spear disappeared, and was instantly wrenched out of Galadus's hand. He spurred his horse on, trampling screaming bodies, and his long cavalry spatha was out, slashing down.

Distant thought was possible, for swinging the sword was automatic. The barbarians were pressed together, and the sheer shock of the charge was enough to pack them so tightly together that they could not raise their arms. A flash of colour passed — a painted shield, a braided beard with grey in it. A chieftain. But he was gone in an instant, trampled under.

There had been no time for the Pictii to count their foes. Suddenly all they could hear were screams, the terrible thud of blows, the trampling of horses' hoofs. On the walls the villagers felt the change. Suddenly the barbarians were turning their backs and struggling to break off.

Galadus could move forward, driving his horse into the crowd of tribesmen, scattering them, trampling them. Knocking one over brought another five or six down under the flailing hoofs, with the long blade flickering like lightning over them. The barbarian battle-cries became wails. Now they were only trying to get away.

Tall columns loomed above him. Here was the centre of the line. The gates sagged but still held, and the walls still stood. Men were leaping down in flight or pursuit, with the flicker of fire behind them. The hall was burning.

Galadus looked around, shaking his head to clear it. The Pictii were running. Everywhere he could see their backs. Among them, like drovers among cattle, his riders slashed right and left, and the barbarians scattered, throwing away shields and spears to run faster.

Galadus swung down and ran for the breach in the walls. He climbed, hard-breathing now, over the rubble. He knew there were too few men to defend the wall properly. Here the barbarians had broken in.

Scattered bodies lay about. A tribesman bent white-faced over a belly wound. Two village men lay dead like kings, spear in hand. And there were screams. The hall.

Other villagers were running towards him, looking wildly around. 'They broke in here,' he called hoarsely. They looked at him as though he had said something mad, then at each other. Clearly, engaged in the desperate fight at the wall, they had never seen the collapse and the break-in. 'Here,' said Galadus, running.

The hall was beginning to burn. Grandfather would be furious, thought Galadus. His furniture, his plate … And then he heard the screams again, and this time it registered.

Perhaps it had been only a dozen or so raiders. Knowing nothing of what was happening behind them, they had broken in. All they knew was that they were the first to the sack. They had made for the hall, of course, thinking their whole tribe was following.

Galadus burst in. It was dark, though the thatch was already burning. He tripped over a body. A woman. There were more screams.

He charged past the fire pit, past the broken high table. The salt dish had been flung against the wall, broadcasting its precious contents. Shouts and screams, from through the doorway.

A woman sprawled on the floor. Others lay still. A man stood with his back to Galadus. Tattooed. A Pict. Starting to turn. There was the trace of a smile on his bleeding face, and Galadus knew, as if informed by God, that the man was about to remark on the spirit of the wench. He held his stroke, so that the barbarian would have a frightful instant of knowledge, and then struck with all his strength.

Another tattooed man ran in through the rear door, shouting something. An alarm. He had realised what had happened. Galadus leaped to meet him, took a thrust on his long shield, and cut in reply. The barbarian stumbled on a smashed leg and fell. Screaming in that same language came from outside.

Smoke was drifting in, and there was an ominous crackling. Galadus sheathed his sword and cast his shield aside. He gestured to the door. 'Out. Get out.' There were three living women, and they stared at him with wild eyes. 'Out,' he said again, and then, inspired, tore off his helmet. 'It's only me. Grandfather sent me. You're needed outside.'

They moved. He turned back, checking. Three women lay dead. There was another, under the body of the first man he had killed. He stooped and threw it aside. Under it ... was Hilde. She was staring, too, but in uncomprehending horror. Her skirts were around her thighs, and there was blood. A livid bruise was forming across her face. Her eyes wandered, unfocused.

He pulled her skirts down, then knelt and scooped her up. Flames were showing now. A man burst in. Beren, wild-eyed. Galadus staggered to his feet. He tottered towards the door, carrying Hilde, and her father stared from face to face.

'My wife is dead. My daughter is shamed.' Beren's voice was a dirge. 'She is a maiden no more.'

'It was not her fault. She was taken by force, and she resisted. The man I killed had her mark on him.' Galadus spoke in a harsh rasp, trying to reach him.

Beren appeared not to hear. Men were carrying water to damp down the smouldering ruins of the hall. Others dug. The bodies must be buried soon, for the weather was warming. 'She is shamed,' said Beren again, drearily.

'Then blame me! I delayed until I was too late to save them!'

Beren said nothing, but his face didn't change. For a moment, Galadus saw the splayed bodies of the women again, and wondered despairingly if the rest of his life would be sufficient to make up for his failure.

Peleus nodded. 'Custom,' he said, and looked at

Galadus. 'Barbarian custom. She now has no bride-right to sell. No morning-gift can be given for her, in compensation for the loss of her virginity. The man who takes her therefore proclaims himself giftless. No man would so far shame himself.' He frowned. 'No man who stands to inherit.'

Galadus shut his eyes. Beren turned to look at him. 'Do you want her?' he asked. 'You can have her.'

For a moment the words were just sounds, a meaningless string of noises. Then Galadus understood. The world dissolved into red raging mist, and his sword was half out before he was even aware of a weight dragging on his arm. Peleus was shouting in his ear, 'No! No! I forbid this. You can do no good —'

'I can show him what I think of his custom!' Galadus knew his voice was a raw scream, and cared nothing. 'And of yours, too, with your columns that gave your house an air.'

He shook the old man off and the sword slid free. The farmer raised dead eyes, but made no other movement, and Galadus saw that Beren would welcome the blade. It whirled up …

'Galadus.' There was something about the calmness of the voice that penetrated even this. 'Do not.'

The sword was still poised, and he stared at Hilde. 'It wasn't your fault,' he said, and that was all he could say.

'No,' she said, distant but clear, though her tears still

fell. 'But it wasn't father's fault, either. Nor your grandfather's. Nor yours. You killed the man whose fault it was, though perhaps in truth it wasn't even his.' She tucked a strand of hair inside her coif, a gesture that tore at his heart. 'No man can help his birth, or the customs of his people.'

He swallowed. 'No.' He looked away. 'We could … that is, will you …?'

'No!' Revulsion sharpened her voice. Then, 'No. That would bar you from your inheritance for good and all.'

'Custom bars me anyway, as your father has just told us.' He paused and she made no reply. 'I think there is more to your refusal than that.'

'Perhaps. And perhaps in time I will forget.' She shuddered. 'Or perhaps not. Even so, I go to no man without right of morning-gift. Never. I am no man's leavings.' Her face took on an inward steel, and then her lips quirked. 'You see, I am bound by custom, too. We all are.'

Peleus had climbed slowly to his feet, helped by his staff. He waited until Galadus had allowed his sword's point to fall to the ground. 'I fear you are right,' he said.

Beren had retreated into his own pain again, and was silent. Peleus watched them and the gulf between them, all three, knowing it was impossible to bridge. 'There is no life here for either of you. It is clear now that Galadus will not be accepted as my heir, and would live as the son of nobody. Hilde would drag out her days as little better than a slave. The courage you have both shown deserves better. Will you allow me to suggest an alternative?'

'Here are the letters,' said Peleus, handing them up. 'My sister the abbess will present you at court when you are of age to be knighted. Hilde will live as a dowered guest, unless she chooses to take the veil herself.'

Galadus, already mounted, took the papers and put them in his scrip. 'I think that is her will.'

'Perhaps. Who can blame her?'

Galadus nodded, said his goodbyes, and clucked to his horse. He followed the horse-litter out of the gate, not looking back.

AUTHOR'S NOTE

Why Galahad? Two reasons: one, that he is usually, and rightly, regarded as the hero of the Round Table most removed from the sixth-century roots of the story, and I wanted to find him a possible place among them; and two, because his distinguishing characteristic, the combination of physical virginity with physical prowess, needs explaining.

So I placed him in the early sixth century, in a world that was palpably falling apart save for an island of order here and there, and tried to explain him in terms that would be plausible then and recognisable now.

Gildas, who of all extant writers was nearest to the actual events, attached even greater opprobrium to the Scotti (then really Irish) and the Pictii than to the Angles and Saxons. The latter two seem to have been mercenary warriors who certainly were happy to take the land, but who at least settled and farmed it, rather than simply despoiling it. The little that archaeology can say about the relations between them and the native British seems to suggest intermarriage and the continuance of community as much as attesting to ongoing strife. I have therefore set my story in a society that was slowly integrating different ideas and values. In time the result of this process would be something greater than the sum of its parts; and the significance of that should not be lost on current Australians.

the plot

Allan Baillie

I am sitting on King Arthur's seat at the Round Table in Camelot, and I can feel the power through my body. I am the only one in the vast hall, but the chairs around me have the shields of all Arthur's knights and just reading them makes me shiver. Lancelot, Gawain, Galahad, Perceval, Gareth, Kay, Hector … And they will have to follow me! Me, Mordred, the son of King Arthur!

There are clanging footsteps from the corridor and I turn to face them.

'Hello, Gwen …?' A tall knight peers around the doorway. 'Not there?' Then he sees me in Arthur's seat and hisses at me.

'Something wrong?' I say.

Lancelot strides towards me. I try to stand up but he is too fast. He seizes me by the scruff of my neck and hurls me into a dark corner. 'This is for great knights, not for boys and pot scrubbers! Get out from this hall!'

I skid onto the cold stone floor and scrabble to get myself on my feet. 'I am a king's son!' I shout.

'Hah!' Lancelot snorts at me like a pig. 'You are nothing but a black sausage made from the plotting sisters of Morgan and Morgause. Arthur has to worry about you but no one else does.'

I shriek in rage, pull my sword from my scabbard and rush at him.

But he doesn't pull his sword to defend himself. He just takes a step quickly toward me, moving under my sword, catching my arm, hurling me back into the corner and walks out of the hall.

'Black sausage!' I slowly clamber to my feet again, slide my sword away and lurch away from the Round Table.

'I am a king's son.' I am spitting the words as I stumble down the corridors of Camelot.

My mother, Morgause, is a queen and I am a son of King Arthur. From a single night. He tries to forget me, but his blood runs in my body. All right, he trembles to hear my name — and he should! I will be the most feared knight in the span of the world and I will tramp the halls of Camelot as its master, but not yet. Not yet …

I knock on the door of Morgan le Fay, my aunt with magic in her fingers.

The door opens, showing Morgan in a silver gown, and she is beautiful as always. She is older than me, older than Arthur, but there are no wrinkles on her face. Her magic is here.

Morgan tilts her head as she looks at me. 'You are having trouble?'

'When, how long?' I grasp the hilt of my sword.

Morgan tingles laughter at me. 'So much hurrying! Be patient, boy.'

'I cannot wait.'

She sighs, shows me into her room and sits in front of a shimmering crystal ball on a small table. 'What happened?'

'Lancelot. Called me a black sausage. I almost killed him.'

Morgan looks up at me.

'Almost.'

'You will. Almost.' She strokes the crystal ball and I watch fiery sparks dance inside.

They say that Merlin taught magic to Morgan, but now I think she has more power than the gibbering old man. She has got his gift of Sight — seeing into the future — and more.

'You will cause Arthur's perfect knight, Lancelot, to

be driven from the kingdom,' Morgan says softy.

'Good!' I punch the air.

'You will deal with Arthur, his Queen Guinevere and his Camelot. You will destroy the glowing castle so completely that nobody will find a stone of it! It says in my crystal ball. I have fixed it.'

For a moment I feel a cold shiver while I look at Morgan's face. I know that she has hated Arthur from the day he was born because he was almost created by Merlin. I know that Merlin caused the death of her father in the making of Arthur and she has never forgiven him. She can't destroy the master wizard but she can destroy his creation, Arthur, with me!

Fine, I don't like Arthur and he watches me like I am a fox in a henhouse, but I never know what is in Morgan's mind and now, that is frightening.

'Well, what will I be doing in the future?' I say.

'In Camelot you will force Arthur to condemn Guinevere to death.'

'Oh, well that's all right.' It's better than that. Guinevere is not my mother and she looks at me as if I am a dung beetle.

'But Lancelot rescues her.'

'Oh. He would, wouldn't he?' I bang the hilt on my scabbard.

'But he has to run away to France, and Arthur and most of the Round Table chase him. So you take over Camelot.'

'Now that's better.'

'When Arthur comes back you have a tremendous battle. So bad the moon glows crimson, the Round Table splinters, Camelot becomes a shattered ruin and you kill Arthur.'

'And *that* is beautiful,' I say softly.

'Yes, it is beautiful,' Morgan says. 'A masterpiece.'

'What happens next?'

'Nothing much, really. I may dance around the cave where Merlin is locked in for eternity ...'

'But what about me?'

'You?' Morgan blinks at me as if she had forgotten who I was. 'Of course you die.'

'Die!' I gasp. 'No, no.'

'Oh yes, yes. As you kill Arthur, he kills you.'

'No, that's terrible.' I shake my head.

'It is a great death. People will talk about it for centuries.'

'I don't care. I don't want to die. I won't do it.'

'But it's in the crystal ball.'

'There has to be another way. Have my stupid half-brother, Gawain, do it instead, or a dragon — there must be a few lying around.'

Morgan shakes her head as she says, 'No, we can't do that.' Then she looks up at me. 'There is something, but it's hard, very hard. No, forget it.'

'No, no, don't forget it. We can do it!'

She gives me her evil eye. 'You don't know what it is.'

'It will be better than killing me!'

'I don't know …' She keeps on looking at me.

'Come on, I am your favourite nephew.'

She sighs. 'Well, we want Arthur off the throne, and you on it, right?'

'Safe.'

'Yes, yes. If this works there will be no battles needed. That's a pity, but that's the way it is.' She strokes her crystal ball. 'With this I can see into the future and as well I can reach back into the past.'

I shrug. 'So? Everyone knows the past, it is done, dead.'

'You are not listening, boy. I see into the future but for a brief moment I can reach back. Not for long, but perhaps enough to alter the pattern of time.'

I begin to understand what Morgan is saying. 'Yes, yes, you can go back and kill Arthur!'

'No, no! We can't kill anything at all when we are reaching, that finishes everything. We can only touch things, objects.'

I shrug. 'What's the good of it?'

'Sometimes I wish I was working with a frog instead of you, Mordred! The frog would be brighter.'

'Leave me alone.'

'Just think. When Arthur started to become a king. The first moment.'

'The sword in the stone! Why, you could —'

'No. It is you who is going back. I don't know

whether this magic works properly and you want to be the king.'

'Well, I don't know …'

But she does it with a wriggle and a wink.

Suddenly I am sprawling across a thorn bush in the first glow of dawn, twenty years back from Camelot. I pull myself from the thorns, swearing, and I reach for my sword to destroy the blasted bush. But my sword is now in Camelot because Morgan insisted that I go back unarmed, just in case.

I kick the thorn bush and walk out of the wood into Westminster. There are many bright tents on the common, flying pennants of noble knights and merchants from the towns and even from countries far away. I can see the lists — low fences — placed in the open for the jousts in the late morning, the horses chomping the grass in a field and finally the glint of the sword under a spreading oak.

I walk quickly across the common toward the sword but I almost trip over a little girl carry a bucket of water. I lift my hand to clout her. 'Wretched brat!'

'Ooer.' She throws her hands up.

'Yes, out of my way.' I decide not to hit her this time.

'You're bleeding.' She catches my hand. 'See.'

'Ooer,' I say. One of the thorns has pricked the back of my hand. I cannot stand to see any of my blood.

'I can fix, I can fix it.' She tows me to a pond and splashed into it.

'Hey, I don't want to get wet.' I pull back.

She slaps strange purple mud onto the back of my hand.

'What on earth are you doing?'

Then she washes the mud away. The blood and the scratch have disappeared. 'Oh.' I know that I'm supposed to say or do something about now, but I'm not sure what. So I look down at this muddy little girl standing in the pond. 'Ah, what's your name?'

'Nynyve,' she says.

'Ninny, whatever. I've got things to do.' I walk away, but I do look back for a moment and frown at the little girl in the pond and the feeling that I should remember her. But there are more important things to worry about so I shrug and turn away.

The sword in the stone is in front of me. Actually, it is sticking out of a black anvil which is locked into a massive piece of marble, but it is a sweet weapon. There are no gems on the hilt, not even a carved dragon, but the blade shines with a deep blue like an Arctic sea.

I wouldn't mind having it … What am I thinking of, of course I will have it! This is why I am here. I read the words set into the marble and shiver a little.

Whoever can draw the sword is
The rightful king of all Britain

We'll see. In about two hours a stupid boy, Arthur, will come to this tournament with Sir Hector and his lump of a boy, Kay, who is about to become a knight. Arthur is nothing, just a carrier of weapons. But he can't even do this. He has forgotten Kay's sword. So he will come rushing past here to get Kay's sword and will see the sword and pull it from the anvil to save time. And that will make him a king.

But not this time.

I move to the sword and give it a tug. It is as solid as a castle, but that's all right. There is a touch of magic on the anvil to make sure no-one can pull the sword out apart from Arthur. But Morgan can fix that problem as easy as a wink. I reach into my pouch for a tiny bottle and tip the purple oil from it where the blade enters the anvil.

There is some crimson smoke coiling from the anvil for a short time and that is all. But that is enough.

I place my hands on the hilt and draw the sword from the anvil as effortlessly as if it were in a silk scabbard. I feel the weight of the sword, smile and look around. There is only a baker, a blacksmith working to start his fire, the little girl and a dark man running around with a low basket. It's not the time now. It's better a little later, in fact much later.

I slide the sword back into the anvil and move away. That sword can make me a king and keep me here instead of shivering back in time to Camelot. The sword now knows me. It will ignore anyone, *anyone*, and stay locked in the anvil until it feels my hand.

I grab a couple of buns from the baker, sit on a log and watch as the crowds trickle in to the common. A couple of jesters start to sing and roll about, and the blacksmith starts hammering a dented suit of armour. Then a few knights clanked past me, laughing at a very old joke, and Arthur comes in with some lances, a mace and two shields.

That odd man with the basket scuttles up to me, touching his turban as he says, 'Have you seen Yasmin?'

'Go away, I'm busy.' I push him sideways so I can watch Arthur.

'Sorry, sorry.' And he shuffles away.

Arthur has disappeared in the crowd but there is a crash through the din, as if someone has dropped some lances, maces and shields. Now is the time!

I stand up from the log and straighten my tunic. I see Arthur hurrying through the crowd, moving closer to the sword, so I walk quickly toward him. He doesn't see me but he sees the sword.

He stops and cocks his head. 'Ah ...' For a moment he is thinking about the sword but then he shakes his head and begins to move away.

He can't do that! I step forward and bump him.

'Oh, sorry,' he says.

'You were looking at the sword in the stone. Maybe you were thinking of lifting it?'

'Oh no, never.' Arthur shakes his head furiously.

I sigh. He is always a pain. 'It's all right. You can take it.'

'Really?'

'Really. All you have to do is pull it from the anvil. You look like you are a strong lad.'

'Well, okay.' Arthur steps up to the sword, flexes his muscles and puts both his hands on the hilt.

At that moment I have a horrible thought. What if Morgan has made a mistake and that sword goes over to Arthur when it feels his hands?

Arthur heaves on the sword. His face becomes purple as he hisses and grunts but the sword sits in the anvil.

I knew that Morgan would fix it properly. 'Having trouble, Arthur?' I say.

'It's stuck.' Arthur stops, panting and looks at me. 'Do you know me?'

'No, no.' I say. You're nothing now. You leave here as just the squire for Sir Kay but maybe I will allow you to live. 'Pull again.'

Arthur shrugs and tries again.

I turn to the seething crowd. 'Hello!' I boom. 'We have a boy trying to pull the king's sword!'

A few people look up and prod a few others.

'Maybe he's the one! The greatest king of them all! He does looks like it, doesn't he? This beardless boy!'

The crowd laughs and a jester pretends to try to pull the jangling hat from his partner. But the little girl stares at Arthur with solemn eyes.

'I can't do it,' gasps Arthur, dropping his hands from the hilt.

'Oh, what a pity,' says Nynyve.

'It can't be too hard,' I say as I step up to the stone. 'Give us a look.'

I put one hand on the hilt and just slide the blade slightly in the anvil.

'Hell!' cries Arthur.

'Yes, you may say that.' I pull the sword from the stone, thrusting it toward the blue sky, the blade flashing in the sun.

The crowd is roaring around me.

'Yes, here is your new king!' I shout as I turn.

But I see Arthur is not looking at me and the crowd is ignoring me. People are pushing each other in front of me, shouting and screaming. The jesters are leaping on top of people's heads and nobody is laughing. Suddenly the crowd had spread from the trampled grass, leaving Nynyve by herself.

'What are you doing, you wretched child!' I shout. After all, this is my big scene. Nynyve jerks her head at me, her eyes huge in a white face, and I realise that she is frightened. Everyone is frightened, including dumb Arthur. Frightened of me and my sword?

Then something black flickers in the grass. Nynyve cries out and leaps behind me.

'What? What is this?' I roar and I pull the sword out of the sky.

Then the black slithering shadow stops and begins

to rise from the grass. It is a cobra. It begins to sway slowly, flaring its wide hood as its glittering eyes hold Nynyve like a rabbit in a cage. It slides toward her, flickering the tip of its forked tongue.

'Do something!' Arthur hisses.

I look at the frightened little girl and remember how she fixed my bleeding hand. 'Oh, get out!' I say and swing the sword at the cobra.

I suddenly realise that I have done the wrong thing. I am watching the blade float down toward the cobra and I cannot change anything now. What did Morgan say about never killing in the past? No matter what.

The dark man has lurched from the crowd, dropping his flat basket and crying, 'Yasmin!'

The blade hits the cobra and at that moment the sword is incredibly heavy in my hand. I stumble and the sword tumbles from my grip, and Arthur snatches it in the air.

'No!' I am shrieking, but nobody is hearing and I am fading away, like mist in the sun.

My last vision of that crowded common is of Arthur frowning at the sword with people cheering. And Nynyve looking at me, where nobody else can see me.

And in the cold tumble back to Camelot I remember who she is. Nynyve, the muddy little girl in that pond, will grow up and become the Lady of the Lake who will give Arthur the mighty Excalibur. Without Excalibur I can whip him and his clanking Round

Table — and that cobra was going to stop that little girl right there.

Worse than all this, I am going back to Morgan and she knows that I have destroyed her diabolical plot by acting like Arthur and saving that little girl. She is going to be very, very angry.

It's not fair.

AUTHOR'S NOTE

I have always been interested in a touch of villainy, and Mordred was a major villain. I mean, he wrecked the love affair between the top blade and the Queen, had her marched to the stake, caused the top blade to flee from the kingdom and burned Camelot. All on the way to destroying the Knights of the Round Table and King Arthur in a terrible battle!

Well, you have to try to work out the mind behind the monster, don't you?

SOPHIE MASSON

Born in Indonesia of French parents, Sophie Masson grew up in Australia and France. A bilingual French and English speaker, with a master's degree in both English and French literature, she is the prolific published author of many novels for children, young adults and adults, with her work published in many different countries. Her latest novels are *The Madman of Venice* (Hodder Children's Books, 2009) and *The Case of the Diamond Shadow* (ABC Books, 2008). Her interest in Arthurian legend is of very long standing, and she has been involved with several Arthurian groups and events. Many of her novels have been influenced by Arthurian themes, and her three-volume novel, *Forest of Dreams* (Random House, 2001) is based on the life and work of the 12th-century poet and storyteller Marie de France, one of the first writers to popularise the Arthurian legend.

Lancelot symbol: Fleur-de-lis in water
The fleur-de-lis is a French royal symbol, denoting Lancelot's parentage, and the water of course is the lake!

MAGGIE HAMILTON

Maggie Hamilton was born at home in a cottage in the North of England on a stormy night. She grew up on the edge of the moors where the old stories had been kept alive. From the moment Maggie learned of Arthur and Merlin these characters and their stories were to haunt her. In recent times she has returned to Britain to recapture the local accounts of Arthur and Merlin in Wales and in Cornwall and Devon. Her books include *The Lost Kingdom of Lantia*, *Mister Eternity*, *Magic Tricks*, *Very Tricky* and *What's Happening to Our Girls?* Maggie now lives in an old terrace in inner-city Sydney with her husband Derek and a mischievous black and white cat.

Merlin's symbol: Blackbird
This symbol has often been associated with Merlin in stories, it is his totem.

JULIET MARILLIER

Juliet Marillier was born in Dunedin, New Zealand. She has worked as a music teacher, opera singer and tax assessor, but is now a full-time writer. Her historical fantasy novels for adults and young adults are published internationally and have won a number of awards. Juliet lives in a hundred-year-old cottage by the Swan River in Perth. She shares her house with a miniature pinscher, an elderly maltese and a tri-coloured cat. She loves history, folklore and travel.

Arthur's symbol: Sword in Stone
The sword Arthur drew from the stone, which proved his kingship.

KATE FORSYTH

Kate Forsyth is an internationally bestselling author of novels for both adults and children. Her books include *The Witches of Eileanan* and *Rhiannon's Ride* fantasy series, *The Starthorn Tree*, *The Gypsy Crown* and *The Puzzle Ring*. She lives in Sydney with her family, a lion-hunting hound, a slinky black cat and far too many books to count.

Morgana's symbol: The Raven

Ravens, birds of magic and death, have long been associated with Morgana.

JANEEN WEBB

Janeen Webb is a multiple award-winning author, editor and critic who has written or edited ten books and over a hundred stories and essays. She is a recipient of the World Fantasy Award, the Australian Aurealis Award, and a three-time winner of the Ditmar Award. She is internationally recognised for her critical work in speculative fiction and has contributed to most of the standard reference texts in the field. She holds a PhD in Literature from the University of Newcastle, and she divides her time between Melbourne and a small farm overlooking the sea near Wilson's Promontory.

Gawain's symbol: the Sun

Gawain is a 'solar hero' whose totem is the sun. In some of the stories it is said his strength waxes and wanes with the sun.

SALLY ODGERS

Sally Odgers was born in Latrobe, Tasmania, and still lives there. She is married to Darrel Odgers, and they have two grown up children. Sally has been writing since the 1970s, and with over 230 books, reckons she's probably Tasmania's most published author. Visit her at home on the web at www.sallyodgers.com

Gareth's symbol: Two Gloves

The gloves that are Gareth's symbol come from one of his traditional nicknames 'Beaumains', which refers to his 'beautiful hands'. No doubt he kept them that way in fine gloves!

Isobelle Carmody

Isobelle Carmody is the award-winning author of *The Obernewtyn Chronicles*, *Dreamwalker*, *Greylands* and *The Gathering* and many other fantasy books for children and adults, as well as short stories. She has one award-winning collection of her own in *Green Monkey Dreams*, and is currently working on another collection to be called *Metro Winds* and the second in *The Legendsong Saga* cycle. Isobelle divides her time between her home on the Great Ocean Road in Australia and her travels abroad.

Guinevere's symbol: Gemini, the Twins
Guinevere is double natured, and in this story, one of the twins.

RICHARD HARLAND

Richard lives in Figtree, south of Sydney, with wife Aileen, cat Habibi and computer (unnamed). His fifteen published novels cover all areas of speculative fiction from fantasy (*Ferren* trilogy) to SF (*Eddon and Vail* series), and from gothic horror (*The Vicar of Morbing Vyle*, *The Black Crusade*) to fantasy for younger readers. His latest novel is the steampunk/Victoriana fantasy *Worldshaker*, which is published by Allen & Unwin in Australia and will be coming out from Simon & Schuster in the U.S. He has won five Aurealis Awards, including the Aurealis for Best Fantasy Short Story (twice) and the Golden Aurealis for Best Novel in any Genre of SF/Fantasy/Horror. He has just put up a free 145-page website of tips for fantasy and genre fiction writers, at www.writingtips.com.au. His author website is at www.richardharland.net.

Iseult's symbol: a Lapdog
In honour of her puppy Tomlin — or is that Dorassy?

URSULA DUBOSARSKY

Ursula wanted to be a writer from the age of six, and has now published over 25 books for children and young adults and won several national literary awards. Her latest book, based on a Tibetan myth and illustrated by Andrew Joyner, is *The Terrible Plop*. She lives in Sydney with her family.

Percival's symbol: Heart on a Shield
To recall the heart-shaped flower left by his father.

FELICITY PULMAN

Knights, ladies, the Holy Grail, the Lady of Shalott and all the romance of Camelot are subjects close to the heart of Sydney author Felicity Pulman. She's so intrigued by the scenes and characters of this bygone age that she visited the UK to walk in the steps of King Arthur and subsequently wrote the award-winning *Shalott* trilogy, published by Random House Australia. Felicity now finds herself 'trapped' in medieval time and is currently working on her medieval crime/romance series for teenagers, *The Janna Mysteries*, also published by Random House Australia. Visit Felicity's website at www.felicitypulman.com.au.

Elaine's symbol: a Lily
In many of the stories, Elaine the Fair is often compared to a lily.

GARTH NIX

Garth Nix was born in 1963 in Melbourne, Australia. A full-time writer since 2001, he has previously worked as a literary agent, marketing consultant, book editor, book publicist, book sales representative, bookseller, and as a part-time soldier in the Australian Army Reserve. His novels include the award-winning fantasies *Sabriel*, *Lirael* and *Abhorsen* and the cult favourite YA SF novel *Shade's Children*. His fantasy books for children include *The Ragwitch*; the six books of *The Seventh Tower* sequence; and the seven books of *The Keys to the Kingdom* series. His books have appeared on the bestseller lists of *The New York Times*, *Publishers Weekly*, *The Guardian*, *The Sunday Times* and *The Australian*, and his work has been translated into 38 languages. He lives in a Sydney beach suburb with his wife and two children.

Nimue's symbol: Star and Stone
To symbolise the important parts played by these in her story.

LUCY SUSSEX

Lucy Sussex was born in Christchurch, New Zealand, and lives in Australia. Currently her day job is writing a newspaper review column. Her writing has been published in a variety of genres, including children's fiction, literary criticism, horror and detective stories. While working as a researcher she solved the mystery of 'Waif Wander' (Mary Fortune), a woman who published 500 detective stories between 1865–1910. She has been a judge for the Tiptree award, and a writer in residence at the Clarion Writers' Workshop in Seattle. In addition she has edited four anthologies, one crime and three science fiction. Of these, *She's Fantastical* (1995) was shortlisted for the World Fantasy Award. She has won Ditmar, Sir Julius Vogel and Aurealis awards, and been shortlisted for the International Horror Guild Award, the Ned Kelly awards (crime) and the Wilderness Society Environment Award for Children's Literature. Her work has been translated into Japanese, Polish, Czech and Russian. At present she is writing *Mothers in Crime*, the story of the mothers of crime and detective fiction.

Minimus' symbol: a Dwarf
Holding up his arm!

DAVE LUCKETT

Dave was born in Sydney in 1951 and moved to Perth in his teens. He took a degree in Medieval History at the University of Western Australia after spending some time knocking around the outback in the late 1960s. Dave has been writing full-time since 1998. He has won two Aurealis Awards and had three shortlistings for the Western Australian Premier's Literary Awards, one shortlisting and five notables on the Children's Book Council of Australia Awards. Dave has had seventeen books published. He is married, with one son.

Galahad's symbol: White Lion on a Shield
This was Galahad's device in medieval stories.

ALLAN BAILLIE

Allan Baillie was born in Scotland, raised in London until he was seven, and then moved with his family to Australia. He went to Victorian bush schools before settling in Melbourne. After school he became a journalist and began writing books. He is now a full-time author, chasing books in Cambodia, China, Arnhem Land and Indonesia. Allan is published in 13 countries with various awards. Married with a daughter and a son, he swims and sails whenever possible. He is always interested in villainy.

Mordred's symbol: a Broken Sword
To symbolise his breaking of Camelot, and King Arthur's reign.

FURTHER READING
AND INFORMATION

Arthurian organisations

International Arthurian Society
website: www.uhb.fr/alc/ias
Publishes the journal *Arthuriana* (details at http://faculty.smu.edu/arthuriana), holds conferences, workshops, seminars, talks and other events. It also has an excellent online discussion group called ARTHURNET which you can join for free, and discuss all sorts of things to do with the Arthur legend! Subscribe by sending a message to listserv@morgan.ucs.mun.ca, containing the message 'Subscribe Arthurnet (your name)', and you will start receiving messages to your email inbox.

The Pendragon Society
website: www.pendragonsociety.org
Established in 1959, this society, based in Britain, investigates Arthurian myth, folklore, archaeology, history, literature and much more. It also publishes an interesting journal called *Pendragon*, to which anyone can subscribe, and every two years holds a special Arthurian event called a 'Round Table' in an area associated with the legend.

Facebook Arthurian Society
If you're on Facebook, you can join the Arthurian Society (just key in those words to search in Facebook). Members can not only discuss Arthurian topics but also post Arthurian essays, articles, pictures, etc.

The original Arthurian texts

There are many versions of the medieval texts of Geoffrey of Monmouth, Chretien de Troyes, Marie de France, Wolfram von Eschenbach, Thomas Malory and so on, mostly in Oxford or Penguin Classics editions. The best place to start, though, is Richard White's excellent compilation, *King Arthur in Legend and History* (Dent, London, 1997), which has extracts from all the major texts, as well as many minor ones, and can be used as a wonderful sourcebook both for the historical and cultural (including legendary) background to the stories.

Modern retellings of the legend

The Story of King Arthur, retold by Robin Lister and illustrated by Alan Baker (Kingfisher Classics, Kingfisher Books, London, 1988). A powerful and comprehensive retelling, based mostly on Malory but taking in other traditions as well, that spares none of the gory or sexy details.

Arthur, High King of Britain, by Michael Morpurgo, illustrated by Michael Foreman (Hodder Children's Books, London, 1998. Also available on audiotape, read by the author.) Another great retelling of the legend (this one was shortlisted for the Carnegie Medal), Morpurgo has a great sense of the beauty and melancholy of the story.

Parzival and the Stone from Heaven, by Lindsay Clarke (Harper Collins, London, 2001). This gorgeous retelling of the story of one of Arthur's most endearing knights preserves the freshness of the original while being told in crystal-clear modern prose. The book also has a very good Preface and Afterword.

The Song of Arthur, by Robert Leeson. This is Arthur as British warrior and chieftain, a moving and powerful evocation of the roots of the legend.

The Acts of King Arthur and His Noble Knights, by John Steinbeck

(Farrar Strauss & Giroux, New York, 1976). This is Steinbeck's beautifully written version of Malory.

The Story of King Arthur and His Knights; The Story of the Champions of the Round Table; The Story of Sir Lancelot and His Companions, all retold and illustrated by Howard Pyle, are available in Dover paperbacks. They are classic editions, beautifully illustrated with line drawings by Pyle, one of the great Arthurian artists of the early twentieth century. The stories are thematically arranged, and Pyle has used all kinds of texts for his collections.

The historical Arthur
The Discovery of King Arthur, by Geoffrey Ashe (Owl Books, Henry Holt & Co, New York, 1987) covers much background, but focuses especially on the Gallo-British lead. Was Arthur really the fifth-century king Riothamus?

Arthur and the Lost Kingdoms, by Alastair Moffatt (Phoenix, 2000). The story of Arthur as a North British chieftain. Focuses on the north of England and southern Scotland.

Arthur the Dragon King, by Howard Reid (Hodder Headline, Australia, 2001). Were the stories of Arthur really of Celtic or of Caucasian origin? Is the Caucasus – Georgia, Iran, Armenia, etc – a better place to look for the origins of the once and future king?

Excalibur: The search for Arthur, by Gwyn A Williams (BBC Books, 1994). This book looks at the Welsh Arthur. It includes much archaeological and cultural evidence, and numerous photos.

The Age of Arthur, a History of the British Isles 350-650, by John Morris (Phoenix, London, 1996). This comprehensive history of a tumultuous period, where the beginning of the stories lie, serves as a useful sourcebook.

General information

The New Arthurian Encyclopedia, edited by Norris J Lacy (Garland Reference Library of the Humanities, 1996) is an excellent, invaluable, and vast reference tool, containing everything you need to know about all aspects of the stories, characters, ideas and manifestations of the Arthurian legend. Includes good sections on film, comics, fiction and so on.

The Illustrated Encyclopedia of Arthurian Legends, by Ronan Coghlan (Element Books, 1993) is also a wonderful book, with exhaustive references to all kinds of Arthurian characters, both major and minor. Beautifully illustrated with gorgeous colour pictures.

The Arthurian Tradition, by John Matthews (Element Books, 1994). Also beautifully illustrated, this book examines the deeper meanings behind the stories and characters.

A selection of novels based on the Arthurian legend
The *Shalott* trilogy by Felicity Pulman (Random House Australia). Based on the doomed love of Elaine of Astolat for Sir Lancelot du Lac, this fusion of contemporary Australia with the world of Camelot brings new insight and meaning to aspects of Arthurian legend. A thought-provoking, moving and exciting timeslip into the legendary past.

The Chronicles of Prydain, by Lloyd Alexander. This beloved five-part series, featuring the adventures of young assistant pig-keeper Taran and a motley collection of friends, started publishing in 1964 with the first book, *The Book of Three*, and has been in print ever since. The books, which are based around the Welsh tales of the Mabinogion, have a strong Arthurian flavour – not surprisingly, as it's in the Welsh stories that a good deal of the Arthurian stories have their roots.

The *Guinevere Jones* books are novelisations of the Canadian–Australian young people's TV series of the same name, which is set around the premise that a young Canadian girl who's just emigrated to Australia is actually the reincarnation of Guinevere. Plenty of wild adventures develop! Based on the screenplays written by Canadian Elizabeth Stewart, creator of the series, the books were written by Australian authors Sophie Masson and Felicity Pulman and follow the characters through the entire series. Published by Random House Australia, they are: *A River through Time*, written by Sophie Masson; *Love and Other Magic*, written by Felicity Pulman; *The Dark Side of Magic*, by Felicity Pulman; *No Place Like Home*, by Sophie Masson.

Forest of Dreams, by Sophie Masson (Bantam Books, Australia, 2001). A trilogy based on the life and work of the great Arthurian medieval poet Marie de France, this is the omnibus edition. Described as a magical medieval adventure, this exciting book takes the reader into the mindset of the Middle Ages and the extraordinary people who made the legend what it was.

The Once and Future King, by TH White (Voyager, Harper Collins, 1996). A beautiful modern classic, this is the omnibus edition of TH White's famous books (there are five in all). Humorous, moving and magical, the books have never been out of print since 1939.

Arthur: the Seeing Stone (2000), *Arthur: The Crossing Place* (2001) and *Arthur: King of the Middle March* (2003) by Kevin Crossley-Holland (Orion Books) is a wonderful trilogy for young people which has been a big international hit. The novels go back and forth between

Arthur of Caldicot, a twelfth-century boy growing up in the Marches (the Welsh Borders), and another boy whose destiny he can see in the stone. Told with verve, robustness, rich detail and humour.

Here Lies Arthur (2007), by Philip Reeve (Scholastic Books). This irreverent take on the story of Arthur, which garnered lots of awards, is set back in the dark and brutal days of the sixth century, and though it won't please everyone, it is a bold and imaginative reworking of the legend which is well worth reading.

More books with Arthurian themes from Random House Australia

CUPID'S ARROW

By Isabelle Merlin

The legends of King Arthur may help Fleur to solve a mystery – and save her life – in this thrilling modern-day fairytale set in France.

It's been a while since Fleur has had one of the nightmares that plagued her childhood. So she's really creeped out when she starts dreaming of being hunted through a dark forest by a sinister archer.

But when her bookseller mother inherits the magnificent library of a famous French author, Fleur forgets about her fears. Excitedly, mother and daughter travel to the ancient French town of Avallon, reputedly the resting place of the 'real' King Arthur. And it is there, in the forest near Bellerive Manor, that Fleur meets a handsome, mysterious boy called Remy. It seems to be love at first sight, beautiful as a dream.

But Fleur's nightmare is just about to begin . . .

Available at all good retailers in August 2009

SHALOTT
RETURN TO SHALOTT
SHALOTT: THE FINAL JOURNEY

By Felicity Pulman

Zapped back in time to the medieval court of King Arthur, Callie and her friends invoke the legend of the Lady of Shalott . . . with terrifying consequences.

'Infectiously readable and admirably comprehensive'
Viewpoint magazine

'This spellbinding story weaves together the past and present to create a tale that is at once dark and dangerous, and tantalizingly dreamlike. *Shalott* is unputdownable.' Maggie Hamilton

'This is an unsettling, unusual, intriguing and moving novel, rich in character, action and mystery, full of the atmosphere of Arthurian legend' Sophie Masson

Available now at all good retailers

For more Random House Australia books, visit
www.randomhouse.com.au

For the best fantasy and science fiction books,
visit www.houseoflegends.com.au